THE POISON CUPBOARD

Hardworking Laura Swanton, a local G.P., has lavished all her affection on her wastrel twin brother. But then he is sent to prison and his wife — of whose existence Laura has been unaware — comes to live with her and her mother. Laura's initial contempt for this woman curdles into vicious dislike, which finally becomes an obsession. Somehow she must avert this threat to the very foundation of her existence. Somehow — but how?

Books by John Burke
in the Linford Mystery Library:

THE GOLDEN HORNS

JOHN BURKE

THE POISON CUPBOARD

Complete and Unabridged

LINFORD
Leicester

First published in Great Britain

First Linford Edition
published 2011

British Library CIP Data

Burke, John Frederick, *1922* –
The poison cupboard. - -
(Linford mystery library)
1. Women physicians- -Fiction. 2. Prisoners'
spouses- -Fiction. 3. Hate- -Fiction.
4. Suspense fiction. 5. Large type books.
I. Title II. Series
823.9′14–dc22

ISBN 978–1–4448–0896–4

Published by
F. A. Thorpe (Publishing)
Anstey, Leicestershire

Set by Words & Graphics Ltd.
Anstey, Leicestershire
Printed and bound in Great Britain by
T. J. International Ltd., Padstow, Cornwall

This book is printed on acid-free paper

For
SAMUEL YOUD

PART ONE

My heart . . .
Still to my brother turns with ceaseless pain,
And drags at each remove a lengthening chain.

1

It was rather like entering a cinema in the middle of a film. She had to piece the story together as well as she could.

Of course there was no doubt about the hero — if one could call him a hero. A hero in the dramatic sense, anyway: the man around whom all this ritual was built. And, to her, a hero in the sense that an adored film star was a hero to so many: she knew that face so well, knew the petulant lower lip, knew every intonation of the voice even though she had not heard it for quite a while.

It was more than two months since they had last seen him. His last letter had been scrappy and inadequate. At times Laura thought about him with that familiar mingling of exasperation and longing; but most of the time she tried not to think. It did no good. He had got away (that was how, wryly, she always put it to herself, knowing that it was his own way of looking at it) and there was nothing to be done. The pain would always be there, but she spent the greater part of her life dealing with pain, real or imagined, and knew a great deal about its comings and goings; knew that to dwell on it was only to intensify it.

She did not encourage enquiries about him. The polite, often gently malicious questions were best ignored.

Unfortunately some of her patients enjoyed mixing gossip and speculation with chatter about their ailments. There were those who had known her since she was a child. They called her, with a hint of patronage, Miss Laura, and considered it their right to probe into family affairs.

It was one such who had led her here. The bland question, 'And how's Mr. Peter getting on these days?' had been the beginning. Laura's remote 'Pretty well, thanks' had been answered by the most casual of references to 'something I happened to see in the evening paper last night,' and after that there had been the call to Dr. Whiting in Jury to ask if he would take any urgent calls which might come in.

And now here she was. She had not been able to get here until after the lunch recess, and she had to pick up the threads. It was not difficult. The whole thing was painfully clear.

A man in a grubby wig rose with an air of confidence which Laura found repulsive.

'As the court has already heard, two of the properties concerned in this case were being handled for the owners by the firm of Thomas Buddington and Partners. I call Mr. Frederick Buddington.'

'Call Frederick Buddington.'

A nervous young man entered the witness box. He glanced unhappily, almost apologetically, at the prisoner in the dock. He answered the preliminary questions regarding his identity and the exact nature of his position in the firm in such a hurried undertone that the judge had to lean forward and ask him to speak up. Buddington blinked, swallowed, and then spoke up in an abrupt roar that sent a titter of laughter round the court.

Counsel said: 'Will you please tell the court, Mr. Buddington, what happened on the afternoon of January 29th of this year?'

'At about three o'clock on the afternoon of January 29th,' said the witness, settling down to something which he had obviously rehearsed with great care, 'a man came in and asked for the keys of two flats we had for rent in the Cromwell Road. He claimed that he had been in two days previously and had been accompanied over the flats by one of our staff. I verified this from our records. He said that he now wished to show his wife over them. I issued the keys to him.'

'Is the man in question in court at this moment?'

'He is.'

'Will you point him out?'

The witness pointed to the prisoner.

'You are quite sure?' said counsel affably.

'Quite sure.'

'You have reason for remembering the prisoner clearly?'

'Yes. I'd seen him before. It wasn't until he came back with the keys that it struck me. And I thought it was a bit fishy that he should be looking at those flats, as he wouldn't be wanting them for himself unless he'd come up in the world a lot lately.'

'What precisely do you mean by that? Had you any particular reason to be suspicious about him?'

'The last time I saw him, he hadn't got much money.'

'What was this last occasion to which you refer?'

'He used to work with one of those shady little agencies that used to fix people up with flats or rooms. Or that's what they claimed. You had to pay a deposit first — but of course there was no guarantee you'd get a room — always some story why there was nothing available, once they'd taken your money off you. They were a disgrace to our profession, and it's a good job that they — '

'My lord, I object.' Defence counsel rose indignantly. 'I submit that these remarks are not admissible as evidence. The prosecution is dragging in matters irrelevant to the present charge in order to besmirch the character of the defendant.'

'My lord, I wish to show evidence of system. The accused claims that he has been working in good faith for his employers. It is part of my submission that he has knowingly practised these shameful deceits, and I can produce witnesses to a series of similar events . . . '

There was a wrangle. The outcome, thought Laura, did not matter. Whatever evidence was relevant or not, whatever was admissible nor not, the truth was plain. She was amazed that the preliminaries had taken so long. The case ought to have been over before she got here. She knew that Peter was guilty. She could have told them that, beyond the shadow of a doubt, he was guilty. Knowing Peter, and listening to the evidence, she saw how it all fitted together — how logically and characteristically it all fitted.

It was a dismal story.

Another witness.

'And the man who, you say, asked for a large deposit for fittings and as a down payment for this flat which, he told you, was so much sought after — is that man present in court today?'

'Yes.'

'Can you positively identify him?'

The pointing finger, the angry righteous voice. 'That rotten, thieving young twister over there . . . '

First the shabby little agency, preying on people who would try anything in order to find accommodation in London. Then, when such agencies ceased to exist, the bolder stroke: the advertisement in the newspaper and the courteous acknowledgment of replies on a finely headed notepaper, the collection of deposits ('Money back if you are not satisfied when you have inspected the house') and the disappearance.

It was quite an accumulation. Taken singly, the various items might possibly have been dealt with in a magistrates' court; added together, they demanded something more than the short sentence a magistrate was empowered to give.

'My lord, I object . . . '

'Similar happenings, your lordship.'

A short debate, and the tussle for

Peter's freedom went inexorably on. Voices talked of abstractions, and it seemed to Laura that they seized every possible opportunity of deviating from the main argument in order to enjoy little skirmishes on the subject of what was and what was not admissible as evidence.

Laura sat with her eyes lowered. To her, only Peter was real. It was nauseating that they should be wrangling over him like this.

Peter ought to have known — known instinctively — that she was here; but he had not once glanced in her direction. She could not bear to look at him, sitting there so blandly. He could hold a pose for an unbelievable length of time: he had looked puzzled and innocent for such a long period now that the most naive jury must surely have realised that he was faking.

She could imagine how easily he had taken money from those house hunters. He would take them along to the house or flat, show them around with his most charming air, and explain so diffidently — so very apologetically, as though ashamed to bring up such harsh matters — how essential it was to put down a deposit these days. It was done everywhere. You simply couldn't get a decent place in town without it. Regrettable, of course, but our firm, like all the others, has to insist on it.

She knew him so well. She knew just how plausible he would have sounded. While he was talking, he would have believed every word he said.

Why argue? Why plead not guilty? The defence was crumbling so easily. There were too many people ready to identify Peter. Too many little flashes of awkward evidence made it clear that his avowed innocence was false.

'The accused is a cruelly wronged man.' Counsel for the defence expressed horror in the hands that rose from his gown. 'Facing this monstrous charge — saddled with the responsibility for the misdeeds of his employers, who have cleverly disappeared — a sincere, hardworking young man . . . A young *married* man, I may add. Ladies and gentlemen of the jury, can you believe that a young

11

man who was himself married only a few months ago would practise such deceit on young couples with whom he must feel the greatest sympathy?'

Married. Peter was married.

The other details of this sordid story had hardly moved Laura at all. They had meant no more to her than so many incidents in their childhood when she had listened to accusations made against Peter — had listened to them and, as his defending counsel then, had lied and argued in his favour. The facts mattered little. What Peter had done meant nothing. He was Peter; faults, failings and petty treacheries added up to Peter; and there was no more to be said.

But now at last she had been hit. The other revelations were nothing: this was a wicked thrust, a blow that physically sickened her.

No word from him for so long. No announcement, not even a casual reference; no invitation; simply a wedding of which they knew nothing — hurried, drunken, in a registry office, reluctantly, indifferently, lustfully? — and his life shared from then on with a woman.

Laura felt no immediate curiosity about the woman. That would come later. For the moment, as defending counsel desperately flourished his oratorical banners before the jury, she felt only that she had been shamefully robbed. She was unable to suppress the sudden trembling of her fingers. It was not the robber who counted: it was the fact of robbery, the awful sense of deprivation.

'Even if we admit that this unfortunate young man was influenced by the bad company into which he had fallen, it is unthinkable that he should be condemned for their faults while they, the instigators, escape. It is unthinkable that . . . '

Hurry, thought Laura. Hurry and get it over with.

She had no doubts about the verdict. It was no good trying to make out that Peter was an innocent young man, or a gullible one. For all the smoothness of his features, he was clearly over thirty, and clearly intelligent — 'A man who ought to know better,' as the judge remarked when passing sentence, adding that he hoped this would mean an end to the appalling sequence of wretched trickeries which had distressed so many people recently.

By the time he had finished, Laura had scribbled a note on a page torn from her appointment book. It went to the clerk of the court, who spoke to the judge.

Permission to see the prisoner before he is sent downstairs. Near relative, a doctor, been out of touch with the prisoner for some time.

Granted.

2

The room was small, and smelt musty. Hopes had died here. The man in blue who sat upright with folded arms on a hard chair in the corner might not have been alive: he was part of the impersonality, the all-pervading deadness of the place.

When Peter saw Laura, his expression snatched at her breath. She felt a constriction in her throat. It was so long since she had last seen him. And yet she knew him as she had never known anyone else in the world. She was at once so close to him, recognising with a stab of pain and love the appealing gesture as he leaned eagerly towards her, his lower lip pouting like a girl's while at the same time his eyes were wary.

He began to speak at once, as though to keep her from reproaching him.

'Laura, you're the last person I expected to see. How did you hear about this rotten mess? It's a bit thick. Don't you think so? You heard the evidence — or what they called evidence? It's really not fair, you being dragged into it, and when the whole thing is so unjust anyway — '

'All right, Peter,' she said. 'All right.'

He stopped. The immediate sheepish smile enraged her and yet was so familiar that she wanted to cry. But she hadn't cried over Peter for years; which meant that she hadn't cried over anybody for years.

He said with exaggerated seriousness: 'How's mother taking this?'

'She doesn't know about it yet. That is, unless some kind friend has been in to tell her — as one came in to tell me.'

'Oh, how rotten, old girl.'

They looked at one another in mute appraisal. They looked, and saw each the same face. Only the woman's hair made any real difference, giving another cast to the features and disguising the outlines. Apart from that they were almost identical; yet where Laura's face was severe and disconcertingly alert, Peter's was somehow lazy and appealing. It was odd. It had been commented on many times by friends and acquaintances when the two were children. Such a shame, it had been generally agreed, that the boy should be so pretty. The girl ought to have had all that charm instead of being such a queer aggressive little thing. She got a reputation for being cold-hearted and even spiteful. Peter was irresistible: even people who distrusted him had to admit that he was hard to quarrel with.

Funny how twins could be so alike and at the same time so different.

But no one could say in so many words just what the difference was. It was something that you recognised after a while — something a very little way below the surface of the echoing faces, looking out from the eyes or caught for a moment in some twitch of the mouth.

Laura said: 'Why didn't you let me know you were in trouble?'

'Oh, you know how it is — '

'I know,' she said, 'that I wouldn't have let you get into such a dreadful mess.'

'Well . . . I didn't like to tell you.

Didn't want to drag you in.'

'If you wanted money, you could at least have told me. It would have been better than this.'

'I've never been a scrounger,' said Peter self-righteously and untruthfully.

She had not asked for this meeting with the intention of abusing him, but love and anger were inextricable. She said:

'I suppose I've always been expecting something of the sort. It was bound to come to it in the end.'

'Aren't things bad enough?' he lamented. 'You don't have to go on at me.'

'I don't see why not. It's what you deserve. You needed it long ago.'

His persistent flickering smile became sly. It was a mark of their estrangement that she could be unsure of the significance of that quirk of the lips. It might mean rueful affection or it might — more probably — be mockery. Perhaps it was silently telling her that she was the reason for his going to live in London after the war, that she was what he had wanted to escape from.

She felt suddenly wretched. She longed

to set him free. Somehow she had failed him. She said: 'Oh, Peter . . . '

'Don't you worry, now.' In a flash he was at his most charming, radiating a glib sincerity. 'Two years isn't so long. And I'll be out before then, anyway. I'll be a good boy and get let out early.'

'How could you have been such a fool?'

'Now don't let's go into that again.'

'But I want to *know*, Peter. I want to understand.'

'Yes,' he said. 'You always did, didn't you?'

The tone of his voice struck into her memory and awoke old responses. She answered as she would have answered years ago, instinctively lunging to throw him off balance. She said:

'What's your address these days — your wife's address?'

'Now look here, Laura — '

'I shall find out what it is somehow. You may as well tell me. I don't imagine it's the same as the old address. I wrote there several times, but you never bothered to reply.'

'Laura, there's no point in — '

'Was she in court today?'

'You don't want to listen to everything a lawyer says when he's up on his hind legs. Just because he put on that sob stuff about me being a married man — '

'Where was she?' said Laura.

Peter shrugged. 'I wouldn't let her come.'

'She does as you tell her?'

'Laura, I'm not going to have you — '

'You must be quite a strong character in your own home,' she said. 'She'll feel lost without you. I'll go and see her, in case there's anything she wants.'

'You're not to,' he cried.

The impassive man in the corner stirred and looked at his watch.

'I won't have it,' Peter went on desperately. 'There's no need for you to do anything, Laura — no need at all.'

'I think I ought to.'

'Please.'

'Why are you so ashamed of her? Why didn't you tell us you were married? Not a line from you.'

'I'm not ashamed of her.'

'Then why — '

'Oh, stop badgering me.'

He sat quite still. Laura waited. She knew she had only to wait. It was to be hoped that the man in the corner would not cut their time short, before Peter had broken down.

At last Peter said: 'You wouldn't understand. We liked being on our own. We didn't want anyone else. We were . . . free.'

'Free to do what? Plan your petty swindles — '

'She didn't know about them,' he burst out. 'She never had any idea.'

'I see. She isn't very bright, I take it?'

'She . . . doesn't think about things. She never asks questions. I used to go out to work, and I brought money home, and that was that.'

'Of course. The respectable housewife getting her weekly allowance from her hard-working husband. Just as it should be.' Laura shook her head wearily. 'Why couldn't you have got an honest job?'

'I had one. But I didn't make enough — '

'She wasn't a good manager?'

The slyness crept back into his eyes. He

looked at her with an expression that was meant to be — what? Philosophic, resigned, vaguely tragic?

'I'm not blaming her,' he said nobly.

'I see.'

'She used to like nice things, and I hated to worry her. When she wanted more money I — well, I just had to find ways of getting it. That's all.'

He looked quietly pleased with himself. Perhaps he would soon be beginning to regret that he had not advanced this defence in court and thrown himself on the mercy of the judge and jury. But here and now, Laura was judge and jury.

'She couldn't help it,' he added. 'She never had any real idea of the meaning of money. I couldn't ask her to economise.'

There was a pause. Then Laura said:

'And her address?'

Peter shrugged. He might have been shrugging responsibility off his own shoulders and on to hers.

'12 Bolingbroke Gardens, W.2,' he said.

The man in blue stood up abruptly. Laura caught her breath. This meant that Peter would be going. He was caught now: he would be imprisoned . . .

And she would know where he was. For the first time in years she could be absolutely sure where he was.

For a second she felt almost capable of tears. Then she was almost ready to laugh, glad that their time was ended. There was nothing she could do here. She saw how Peter was studying her, wondering whether she was now prepared to stop criticising him. He had always longed for other people's respect.

She said: 'Well, I've got to go.'

'You'll write?'

'You haven't paid much attention to the letters I've been sending you the last couple of years.'

'I shall have more time for reading now,' he said boldly.

She put out her hands as though to make one last claim on him. Then she left, and went off in search of his wife.

Outside, she felt as a drunkard might on emerging into the fresh air. She swayed, and made an effort to walk very slowly and deliberately. Memories of Peter at home, Peter reading cheap magazines and smiling sly complicity at her when she caught him, Peter swimming at Tapton Harbour and sneering at a boy friend she had once had, Peter contemptuously describing his girl friends to her . . . all these and so many more surged up in her mind and blotted out the present reality of London.

She stopped, and stared with determination across the street until everything came clearly into focus.

This was — she must force herself to realise it — like all her previous visits to London: so much to be done in such a short time. She had to hurry from one place to the next without pause, doing things swiftly and systematically, not stopping to think until she was in the train going home.

It had always been like this, and today of all days it was better so.

3

The house was on the corner of the square. The buildings enclosing the square were tall, so that the tattered grass plot and dingy flowerbeds in the centre were sunk in gloom. Each house had a massive portico with a number painted on the pillars. One or two had been recently painted, so that they stood out from the others with an elegance that was very nearly ostentatious. Most of the pillars were stained, and flakes peeled from them like sunburnt skin; but there had been very little sun here.

A polite little man with dark features opened the door just as Laura was about to press the button marked 'Swanton'. He directed her to the first landing, and she went up. From behind the door he had specified came the urgent chattering of a radio.

Laura knocked. The radio continued, bursting into a flourish of music.

She knocked again.

This time the door opened, and it was as though the volume control of the set in the corner had been sharply turned up. She had difficulty in making herself heard; and added to that was the difficulty of forcing out those opening words:

'Mrs. Swanton?'

'Yes.'

'I'm Laura Swanton.'

'What did you say?'

'I said I'm Laura Swanton. Peter's sister.'

'Oh.' The pale brown eyes widened. 'Oh. Come in.'

Laura walked into the uproar. Peter's wife looked at her blankly, and then at the radio, as though reluctant to switch it off even now. Then she gave a shrug, and went and flicked the knob.

The room was far more attractive than one would have guessed from the exterior of the house. A tall window opened on to a balcony — over the porch, Laura realised — and there was a surprising sensation of brightness in the room. The radio was large and new, almost certainly expensive. The furniture was badly chosen, but it was not cheap; or, rather, some of it was cheap but other items were very good and quite incongruous. One had the impression that things had been bought on impulse, taken from their setting in some decorous shop and set down here with blithe indifference to any clash of styles.

Newspapers and magazines were stuffed down the sides of chairs. A pair of stockings had been dropped in the middle of the carpet. A cup smeared with lipstick and coffee stains stood on the tiles before the gas fire.

'I was just tidying up,' said the girl vaguely.

Laura sat down, deciding that there was no point in waiting to be asked.

She said: 'You've heard the verdict?'

'The woman from downstairs went. She phoned me.'

There was a pause.

'Peter didn't tell me your name,' said Laura.

'Charlotte.' Then she added defiantly:

'Charlotte Swanton.'

'You *are* married?'

The girl did not flare up. Indeed, a sort of distant amusement glowed for a second through her dazed expression. She might have been on the verge of a giggle. 'Oh, yes,' she said.

'Sorry. But knowing Peter . . . Anyway, I'm Laura. I thought I'd better come and see you.'

'Yes. Of course.'

Then Charlotte burst into tears and sat down.

She was, Laura judged, some seven or eight years younger than Peter. Twenty-five, say. The wide eyes made her look childish and incredibly naive; but there were also little clusters of wrinkles in their corners, and at the corners of her mouth. As she cried she screwed up her face so that ridges creased her whole forehead. Obviously she used her features too much, too intensely: in ten years' time she would look quite old, because she was so intense in every emotional outburst.

Laura said: 'I just want to know what help you're likely to need.'

Charlotte fumbled for a handkerchief. She could not find one. Her fingers groped blindly down the side of her chair, and still she did not find one.

'Here you are,' said Laura.

'Thank you. Oh, I feel so dreadful.'

'Because Peter's gone to prison,' said Laura quietly, 'or because you had something to do with it?'

Charlotte dabbed at her eyes, blew her nose, and stared.

'Whatever do you mean? I didn't know anything about it.'

She was pretty. Jealousy bloomed more and more luxuriantly within Laura as she saw and admitted it. The girl was pretty. The sort of prettiness that would not last. It depended so much on that smooth plumpness of feature and fresh colouring to which time was so merciless — so swiftly and unexpectedly merciless. The brown hair, just brown and nothing more distinctive, was fluffy and attractive now. It was too long, but clearly the girl was vain, and for a few more years would have cause to be. After that, she would look very ordinary.

But at least she would have had those few years. She had already known years such as Laura had never known. And what use had she made of them?

Laura said: 'How did Peter come to drift into this sort of trouble? Couldn't you have looked after him better?'

'But I didn't know. I had no idea . . . '

'You couldn't have been very observant.'

'He always seemed so cheerful. There was never anything — '

'I always knew when he was up to something,' said Laura. 'I could always tell at once.'

'Yes,' said Charlotte with a wan little smile; 'so he mentioned.'

'We were very close. No one else could understand how close we were. It could never be the same with anyone else.'

Charlotte crumpled up the handkerchief Laura had given her and pushed it down behind her chair cushion.

'I had no idea,' she repeated. 'He never told me what he was doing. He just brought money home every week and gave it to me — '

'And you spent it.'

'Of course. That's what it was for. We liked having nice things. We liked having a nice time.'

Her eyes filled again with tears.

'And what are you going to do now?' Laura demanded bleakly.

'I don't know. Oh, it's awful. I just can't think. Why he had to go and do this . . . He oughtn't to have let me in for this, it wasn't right.'

'You've got a job of your own?'

'Not really.'

'What do you mean?'

'Well . . . I did a bit of typing for people every now and then, but nothing regular. I could never settle to hammering out page after page of stuff — I haven't got the temperament for it. And Peter liked to find me here when he got home. You never knew when he'd come. Often in the middle of the day. And when he got here, often . . . ' The anguish of the sensual recollection seemed to broaden her features. Her lips parted. 'Married women ought to stay at home anyway,' she said despairingly.

31

Laura glanced round the disordered room. A door stood ajar, and through it she glimpsed dishes piled on a small drainboard. She said:

'What do you do all day?'

'Lots of things.' Charlotte was defiant. 'I read a lot. We always get lots of books every week.'

Books. She meant, of course, magazines.

'This place must be quite expensive,' said Laura.

'It is.' There was pride in her voice. 'It's an awful lot. But as soon as I saw it I said we simply had to have it — '

'And that's why Peter is where he is now.'

There were more tears. Laura sat back. She was a prosecuting counsel. Here was the real culprit, the one who ought to have been in the dock: here the criminal whose folly and extravagance had led Peter into trouble.

'And I suppose,' Laura went on, 'you have a lavish wardrobe. You spend quite a fair amount on clothes, I imagine.'

'He always liked to see me looking

nice.' Charlotte made a great effort to gain control of herself. 'And what business is it of yours? What right have you to come here and blame me for all this? I don't have to say anything to you.'

'I'm his sister,' said Laura. 'He means a lot to me.'

'Do you think he doesn't mean anything to me?'

'I really can't imagine,' said Laura with what she knew to be childish brutality. She took a deep breath. 'What are you going to do now?' she asked again.

The reply was the same. And Charlotte looked at a picture on the wall ahead of her as though she could not believe that she would have to leave here. It was plain that she would make no move of her own accord.

Laura said: 'You're Peter's wife, so it's up to us to do what we can for you.'

'I'm not asking for charity.'

'In that case, what exactly do you propose to do?'

Charlotte slowly said: 'Why do you hate me?'

'I suggest,' said Laura, 'that you move

into a smaller place — a bed-sitting-room, or something — and try to get a job.'

'Is it,' said Charlotte, 'because you know that I can give him . . . give him something that you never have and never will?'

Only from her eyes was it discernible that Laura had heard. She went on:

'Whether you get a job or not, I'll make sure you get some money each week.'

'I don't want — '

'Just to keep you going until Peter comes out of prison and decides what he's doing to do next.'

'Peter,' said Charlotte.

It was not an appeal, not even a cry of despair: it was only a sound without echo.

Laura got up. Her brisk, significant movement was known to many a patient who had stayed too long, or who had kept her at a bedside with garrulous lamentation.

'You'll have some tea?' said Charlotte vaguely.

'No, thank you.'

'Next time you come, perhaps.'

Laura led the way to the door and

opened it while Charlotte was making ineffectual lunges for the knob.

Laura said: 'Well . . . '

With an effort she put out her hand.

'Don't think awful things about me,' said Charlotte suddenly. 'I don't see why you have to. He's to blame, if anyone is. But I don't blame him. I'm not that sort. I loved him. And he loved me. And it's still the same. Doesn't that mean anything to you?'

There was no answer. There could be no answer.

'No matter what's happened,' said Charlotte, her face twisted, 'it was beautiful . . . '

She leaned on the door. Beyond her, Laura had a last glimpse of the bright, crumpled covers of magazines protruding from everywhere.

That last declaration remained with her like a sweet cloying taste in her mouth as she went out into the square.

Now she hated the creature more than ever.

To have that voice and that shoddiness and sentimentality always near one . . . It appalled her that Peter should have been able to endure it, and yet she knew too well that it was just the sort of thing he would find endearing. He would have coped happily with the swing between whining and ecstasy; he would have sunk comfortably into disorder, and would have aroused himself only when she nagged or insinuated or wept that she wanted more money, a new coat, an evening out. They must have fought a lot; but Charlotte's skirmishes with him and the subsequent reconciliations had achieved more for her than anything Laura could ever have won from Peter. It was degrading to consider it.

If I had that creature in the house, she thought, I wouldn't be able to stand it. She'd drive me to distraction.

It was all of a piece. It was all characteristic of Peter, of his defection, his repudiation of Laura.

Yet still it was Peter who mattered. Somehow, some day, she would reclaim him. Sitting in the train, she knew that there must be a way and that she would in the end find it.

4

A week later, Mrs. Swanton went up to London and fetched her daughter-in-law back to Brookchurch. She said nothing to Laura about it. She waited until Laura was out on a series of visits, and impulsively went.

Someone had to do something about that poor girl, all on her own. And besides, Mrs. Swanton wanted to see for herself what the child was like. It was all very well for Laura to say how impossible she was. That was just like Laura: she had been like that about every friend Peter had ever had. In fact, it was the way Laura had gone on about this girl that drove Mrs. Swanton herself to go and see her. And having seen her, she simply had to bring her back. She couldn't not bring her, after seeing what a state she was in.

After all, she was Peter's wife. A nice little thing, in her way. Mrs. Swanton thought she was going to like her. It was nice to do what was right — even Laura would have to admit it was right — and get something pleasant out of it as well. It would be someone to talk to. She could tell that Charlotte was the sort who would like talking and being talked to. Such a change from Laura.

Strangely, Laura made hardly any protest at all. When the two of them came apprehensively in, Laura looked almost as though she had been expecting this to happen. There was quite a strange expression on her face. Her mother had not known what reception to expect. She had certainly not anticipated this: not this queer resignation, this tranquillity.

5

It had taken only that one week to reduce Charlotte to despair. Not savage despair, and not a crumpled tearfulness: rather was it a state of complete withdrawal, a refusal to believe that life would go on or that there was any point in its going on anyway.

She had been alive, surely, before she met Peter? She tried to remember what it had been like. Often in those eighteen months of their marriage she had told him that she couldn't imagine why she had married him. And she had meant it; but now she could not imagine the days and nights without him.

There would be so many of them.

Charlotte had never been able to envisage the future beyond tomorrow, or perhaps the day after tomorrow. A week hence was a remote and improbable time. Now she was faced by inapprehensible months.

At first she was sustained by anger. For two days she carried on a long argument with him, although he was not there. She rehearsed accusations and delivered them resoundingly, without saying a word aloud. She had often done this before. While he was out she would shuffle round the flat, working up some grievance until it was ready to explode. She anticipated his answers and twisted them to her own use. Sometimes the fury had abated by the time he got home; at other times, he would walk uncomprehendingly into a downpour of lamentation. He was skilled at dealing with this after a while. But now he was not here to answer, and would not be back for a long time.

How could you have left me in this mess? Always the same, doing something stupid and saying nothing about it. Now what am I to do? It's your responsibility. All of it's your responsibility. I'm your wife, you ought to have thought of me. And don't say I'm extravagant, because I'm not. What about those new shirts of yours, those ties you didn't need, the painting you bought and the cuff-links? If

I spend anything, it's because you expect me to. If I'd known how difficult you were going to be, I wouldn't have been such a fool as to marry you . . .

She paced up and down, snatching up film magazines and dropping them again, so that when she walked back across the room she was treading on creased pages and kicking magazines ahead of her. A full-page photograph of a Hollywood star yearned up at her, half obscured by the smirking features of a coy face on the cover of a woman's weekly.

Charlotte kicked the woman's paper aside and peered down into the soulful eyes below.

Then her mood gradually changed. She visualised Peter staring out between bars, just as in an American film, and she longed to reach out and touch him. I'll be waiting. We'll begin a new life. All will be forgotten, and when you're back with me we'll both be different. I don't mind being poor, so long as we're together.

They would walk off into the sunset.

Slowly that mood, too, left her. She sat then for long stretches of time and stared into the gas fire. She was not now recalling old arguments or happiness: she was numb, remembering little, aware only of loss. She was cold. It was the sort of chill you couldn't get rid of by turning up the fire or drawing the curtain across the door. It was just there. You didn't do anything about it. You didn't do anything about anything.

In her more wakeful periods she cried sometimes, but not with any real fervour. She had cried more readily and with more enthusiasm when she and Peter had been fighting, and then recovered quickly.

What she missed most was his dependence on her. No one could have said she mothered him. That wasn't what he wanted; he would have shied away from it. She had been, rather, the irritation which kept him going, giving him purpose and vitality — vexing him out of his laziness, so that even when he was shouting at her she knew that he relied on her.

She wanted him back. She wanted to hear him making a fuss about something, going off into one of his petulant rages.

One morning she could no longer be bothered to get out of bed. She lay there till noon, got up for an hour, and then went back. She did not sleep but she was not truly awake. Soon she would have to make decisions; but now she wanted to postpone them. All their decisions had, until now, somehow made themselves: she and Peter had talked at cross-purposes, or spat abuse at one another, or made love, and somehow in the end they had known what they proposed to do. Now she had no one to rasp against.

She was waiting. She had no idea what she was waiting for.

Then Mrs. Swanton arrived.

Charlotte never analysed people. She liked them or she didn't like them. 'I can tell at first sight whether I'll get on with them,' was her boast. It took a lot to make her change her mind about anyone after that first sight.

She liked Mrs. Swanton.

She saw her as a plump, faded woman with a funny little mouth. Her feet were remarkably small — too small for her podgy body, so that she did a quick, jerky waddle as she moved along. She seemed to be on the verge of falling over as she came into the room, rather like a dog whose hind paws rush out of control and threaten to catch up with its forepaws.

'So you're Charlotte,' said Mrs. Swanton, and kissed her.

At once Charlotte sat down and cried.

'There, now,' said Mrs. Swanton, delighted.

She did not look round the room as her daughter had done. The litter, which had certainly increased since Laura's visit, left her quite unperturbed: indeed, her first reaction was that this was such a cosy little place. She stood over Charlotte and patted her head, and felt that this was all just as it should be.

'Oh, I'm so ashamed,' sobbed Charlotte when at last she could speak. 'I don't know what you must think of me.'

Mrs. Swanton's thoughts were in fact pleasant ones. She said:

'I just had to come and see you, my dear. I'm so sorry Peter never brought you down to visit us.'

'He never would. He was . . . scared.'

Mrs. Swanton nodded, jerkily, like a bird. 'Of Laura. Yes, of course. I know just how he felt.' She had reason to know how he felt, poor boy.

'I don't know what I'm going to do,' said Charlotte.

It was not often that Mrs. Swanton was in a position to make decisions. Usually they were made for her. Her son had gone away, and her daughter gave instructions instead of taking them. Now, here, at last, was someone who needed help.

She said: 'You're coming back with me.'

'Oh, but I couldn't.'

'It'll be lovely having you.'

'But I can't leave here.'

'Can't you?' said Mrs. Swanton happily.

Charlotte rubbed her eyes and saw the room through a blur that made it foreign and unreal. Of course she could not stay here. But she said:

'Well, I can't just come down and stay with you. What would I do?'

'We'll find something. What you need first of all is a good rest. And when you're ready for a good long talk, we can have one. Now you get packed up right away' — once she was started, there was no limit to her daring — 'and just come away and leave everything. We can always decide what to do about this place later.'

That was what they did. If Mrs. Swanton began to have misgivings on the train and to wonder how on earth she had managed to do so much in such a short time, she did not convey this to Charlotte. Charlotte sat looking out of the window, watching London peter out against a hillside as the train entered a tunnel. On the other side was a broad valley into which they raced with gathering speed, and then another tunnel. She began to feel that she was a long, long way from Peter by now.

She and Mrs. Swanton talked without saying anything of any consequence. They both derived a great deal of pleasure from it.

And so Charlotte came to Brook-church.

'Just you take everything easy for a few days,' said Mrs. Swanton. 'Then we can talk things over and get it all settled.'

Laura used a similar phrase. 'When you feel a little better, we can see about getting things settled.' But there was something more ominous in her voice than there had been in her mother's

Charlotte decided not to think too much about this. She would heed the part about taking things easy and waiting until she felt better.

6

She took things easy. She stayed in bed late in the morning, listening to the wind that blew in from the sea or the rain against her bedroom window. Mrs. Swanton insisted on her staying as late as she liked, and obviously derived intense enjoyment from running up and down stairs to her, although she was out of breath each time when she reached the landing.

The bedroom looked down the garden to where, beyond the fence, the level fields unrolled towards the sea. At this time of year they looked grey under the sullen sky, and the thin line of water a few miles away was cold grey in keeping with them.

'Wait until we really get the spring,' said Mrs. Swanton. 'Signs of it already. You wait and see. It's such a bright room, this one — lovely and bright.'

Charlotte sat propped against the

pillows, contemplating the striped and flowered wallpaper with warm satisfaction.

'Was this Peter's room?' she asked.

'No. Laura's got that. It's at the front,' she added, as though that explained Laura's need for it.

Charlotte said: 'Is it nicer at the front than it is here?'

'No. Laura just . . . well, she just insisted on moving into it when Peter went away. She still keeps all their old toys and books and things. It's funny. But there, that's her way . . . '

In this room there were none of the odds and ends to which Charlotte was accustomed. The furniture was straight and square, lined up in rather military fashion. The lace mats on the dressing-table — a heavy old piece with side mirrors that swung slightly, creakingly towards you if you pulled out the top drawer — were set out with mathematical accuracy, and were not stained and crumpled as Charlotte's had been. There was nothing here like her collection of pots, tubes and bottles. Of course, when all her things came down from London she could make the place look different. There was no pouffe, and no thick rug. There was no gas or electric fire; the fireplace was an ornate iron one, the grate itself being filled with logs and fronted by a neat paper frill. It was austere, and could have been depressing. But Charlotte liked it.

'This is . . . the real thing,' she said on her second morning, not knowing exactly what she meant.

'Yes,' agreed Mrs. Swanton, as though she understood.

When Charlotte got up in the morning, she could hear voices downstairs. At intervals there would be the thump of the front door. That was, explained Mrs. Swanton, the sound of patients coming into the waiting-room.

Their voices would buzz or grumble as Charlotte went downstairs and past the door of the consulting-room. Sometimes she would hear a baby whimpering or someone coughing persistently.

On the fifth morning, Laura was waiting at the foot of the stairs as

Charlotte came down. She was wearing her coat loosely and carrying a doctor's bag. The intersection of light from the hall and from her open consulting-room door struck shadows across her face. It was so like Peter's, that face: odd that it should be so like it and yet so plain. Charlotte knew that Laura must be thirty-two, because Peter was thirty-two and they were twins; but she looked forty if she was a day. Her hair all plastered down on her head, and grey in that miserable light. And where her face wasn't streaked with shadow, it was shiny and well-scrubbed.

Charlotte said: 'Hello, Laura. I haven't seen much of you.'

'I didn't think your case was serious enough to warrant medical attention.'

'No, of course not. I didn't mean that. Really, I know it's dreadful, the way I've just been — '

'One thing I wanted to ask you,' said Laura, buttoning up her coat with one hand. 'Do you think you could be a bit quieter when you get up in the mornings?'

'I'm sorry. I didn't know — '

'I like the place to be reasonably quiet when I'm doing surgery. Patients don't like people clumping up and down when they're telling me things in confidence.'

'Of course. I'm sorry. I will try.'

Laura went out. The door slammed behind her, so that the whole house seemed to quiver for a moment. Charlotte was sure that this was a sign of bad temper; but in the course of the next few days she realised that Laura always twitched the door behind her and let it slam in that way.

She was glad that Laura was so busy. There were morning and evening surgeries, and during the day she was out most of the time on visits. In the evening there were nearly always telephone calls, and out she would go again. It was rarely that Laura spent an hour in the company of her mother and sister-in-law. Charlotte was sure that one day soon she would get a lecture from Laura, full of stern advice and awkward questions, but it would not come until Laura had more time to spare. Charlotte and Mrs. Swanton could get along very well without her. They made innumerable cups of tea, and Mrs. Swanton told Charlotte all there was to know about the people of the district.

In the afternoons she occasionally went out for a walk. But not far.

She would close the heavy front door quietly behind her. Only Laura was allowed to slam it. Then she would stand there for a moment with her back to it. Once she felt suddenly guilty, realising that she was obliterating the two brass plates on the door, and she moved hastily to one side so that anyone who was coming looking for the doctor would be able to recognise the house.

The plate on the left was rubbed and worn, the lettering almost illegible from constant polishing. That on the right was still new — so new that you didn't take it quite as seriously.

REGINALD SWANTON   LAURA SWANTON
M.B., F.R.C.S.   M.B., B.S.

'Of course, it was hard lines on the old man.' She could hear Peter saying it as clearly as though he stood beside her; as though the house itself contained so many echoes of his voice that his remembered words were at once amplified and revitalised. 'He wanted me to follow in his footsteps, but . . . well, I was never any good at that sort of thing. Couldn't stand it.' Peter could not stand the sight of other people's injuries. Although he had not done more than wince when he cut his hand on one occasion, and had been stoical over the pain when he had trapped his finger in a closing door, he would turn pale at the sight of blood on anyone else. When one of Charlotte's nails had broken off he had almost been sick. 'Poor old Dad — in the end he had to make do with Laura. But I suppose he'd be proud of her now: she's certainly carrying on the old tradition.' He had expressed no regret: until now, this house and the sister who was a doctor had been rather unreal to Charlotte — the sister a bit of an ogre, from whom Peter had fled, and the house just a house. Now it was all imposing and real, set down solidly in the middle of this alien landscape.

Brookchurch stood in the heart of marsh-land reclaimed from the sea so many centuries ago that there seemed no reason why the name of marsh should have stuck to it. Two roads met at Brookchurch, one swerving away to the east, the other making its way towards the sea in a vague south-westerly direction. Ditches squeezed themselves into narrow pipes under the roadway and emerged on the other side to spread out around tall sibilant reeds. They converged on small sluices and separated again; they marked out fields, taking on the function of hedges. In summer they were choked with a luxuriance of mallow; in winter there was a glow of heliotrope above the cold black and green water. Up and down the low humped backs of the dykes scrambled sheep innumerable, cropping away insatiably at the grass, adding the sound of crisp moist crunching to the other small unceasing noises — the persistent lark, the melancholy plover, the occasional heavy flapping of swan's wings, a chattering in the grasses, a plopping and restlessness in the ditches — that somehow all added up to an impression of clear, spacious silence.

At first Charlotte found the marsh hostile. It was too flat and went on for too long. She felt that if she walked too far out on it the whole thing would tilt and tip her off into the sky. When the clouds parted to allow a wintry brightness into the afternoon, the sky was so remote that it made her dizzy. There was nothing to protect one, nothing along the edge of the world to prevent a fall over that edge.

Then, gradually, it began to appeal to her. The indeterminacy of the roads suited her: she hated dead, straight roads that went on and on, bullying and powerful in their decisiveness. Here, everything was leisurely and, in a way, pleasantly stubborn. In summer it would be a lazy world. She could feel it. They had a foretaste of summer one afternoon when the sun flooded the marsh and filled the house with brightness from all sides. The face of the church clock shone. In high summer it would be wonderful. Charlotte yawned and stretched in warm anticipation.

But something would surely happen before summer came. Laura would surely have a word with her — drop hints about getting a job, or something. No, not drop hints: Laura would come right out with it.

Charlotte began to rehearse arguments, working herself up into an anger. It was difficult. She did not know the workings of Laura's mind as she had known Peter's.

One morning she came downstairs to find Laura drinking a cup of coffee before going out on her rounds. For once she did not appear to be in any hurry. It was impossible to retreat, although Charlotte felt an immediate urge to do so.

Instead, she found herself anticipating the challenge which was certain to come now.

'Hello, Laura. I suppose I ought to be thinking of getting a job.'

Laura's thin eyebrows rose quizzically. 'Oh. Why?'

'Well, because . . . I can't just hang about here like this.'

'Can't you?' There was something insulting in Laura's indifference.

'It won't do,' Charlotte rushed on. 'I mean, I can't eat your food and just do nothing. There must be some work I can do.'

'I understood you were helping Mother about the house.'

'Oh, yes, but I ought to do something else as well.'

'There's no need.'

Charlotte sat down at the kitchen table, not sure what to say next.

'Coffee?' said Laura.

She got up, and while Charlotte was saying, 'No, you sit down, it's all right, let me get it,' she had poured more coffee into a cup and set it in front of Charlotte.

'There must be something I can do to help you,' said Charlotte at random.

'You wouldn't by any chance be a qualified dispenser?'

'No.'

'I didn't think so.'

'But there must be *something*.' Why was she insisting? She couldn't stop herself. Laura's indifference was drawing it out out of her.

'You needn't worry.' Laura looked down into her cup with narrowed eyes, as though squinting at a microscope slide.

'You're Peter's wife. You can stay as long as you like.'

Charlotte felt herself flushing. Her eyes stung. She wanted to spit back, to lead Laura into a fight as she had so often led Peter into one. But it would not, could not be the same. She felt baffled and impotent. There would be no satisfaction, no final resolution of an argument with Laura: Laura was somehow not human.

'If you're bored,' said Laura slowly, 'you can come out with me in the car, while I do my visits. I could leave you down at Tapton Harbour while I run along the coast road. I've got to see old Drysdale about his leg, for one thing. An hour is just about enough for a visit to Tapton Harbour.'

'It's not that I'm bored.'

'It'll do you good to have a run.' Now she was sounding professional — dictatorial, even. 'It's not going to be a bad morning. Come along.'

'But my clothes — '

'Are perfectly all right. This isn't Piccadilly.'

If the remark implied anything, it was

best left alone. Charlotte looked down at her blue slacks and sweater. 'At any rate these are warm.'

'Of course they are. Get your coat, and we'll go.'

They went.

At the end of the main street the road turned at a sharp angle below the Norman tower of the church and ran almost parallel with the coastline. There were no hedges; only an occasional outcrop of black and white fencing to mark a dangerous corner. The marsh roads were level but not straight. The one which they were on now followed an old dyke: prodded aside by old boundaries, it pursued an erratic course, turning and meandering with a perverse indifference to destinations.

'The ranges are over there,' said Laura, nodding towards a yellow line of shingle in the distance. 'They still do some firing.'

'Is that where we're going?'

'Not today.'

The sensation of dream-like infinity settled down once again on Charlotte. The humped towers of the lonely churches turned slowly and incessantly, maintaining an exasperatingly even distance from the car, which seemed to be getting nowhere. The earth revolved, the land began to rock, and the whole landscape tilted dizzily under the vast sky.

Laura said: 'Nasty roads at night. Quite a lot of accidents during the war. Army drivers on the way to the ranges used to overshoot these corners and finish up in the ditch. It's easily done.'

'Do you have to go out a lot at night?'

'Sometimes. I know the district pretty well by now.' Laura drew up outside a farmhouse, and cut off the engine. Silence rushed down on them. 'Even if you're only walking, you need to be careful.' she said, reaching for her bag from the back seat. 'People have been known to walk into a ditch and get tangled in the weeds.'

The wind began to hum in the telegraph wires. Charlotte watched Laura walk up to the side door of the farmhouse and knock. It opened, and she went in.

The bonnet of the car creaked as it cooled.

If this was a dream — and the landscape was as strange and expansive as that in a dream — there was something frightening in it. Charlotte wanted to run away. Her fear was a nameless one, nagging at the back of her mind. But the desire to escape was a lazy desire, without much conviction behind it; and besides, how could you run across those endless fields? On and on, until you reached the edge . . . and turned to find someone close behind you.

She blinked and made an effort to wake up. But she was already awake, and nothing altered.

She wondered what she was doing here and why Laura had troubled to bring her out. There was no way of telling. You couldn't begin to understand Laura. Like so many doctors, she had a glazed surface. That was it: a glazed surface.

Laura came out and slid back into the car.

'Everything all right?' asked Charlotte timidly.

'He's got about three months,' said Laura, flicking the ignition key. 'Or less, if he's lucky.'

'Oh. How dreadful.'

'It's amazing,' said Laura conversationally, 'how people ignore things they've been told about so often. Goodness knows it's been dinned in often enough, even in the popular papers — if you've got a small lump that doesn't hurt, go and see a doctor about it. But they won't. They pretend it's not that *sort* of a lump. And by the time they do call you in . . .' She shrugged.

'Will it be painful?'

'It's painful already. It won't get any better.'

'Couldn't they do anything for him in hospital?'

'I'll get on to them as soon as I get back to see when they can admit him. But there's precious little hope for him.'

Charlotte trembled. She was like Peter, afraid of other people's pain. She glanced back at the house as they drove away, and the eroded brickwork on the seaward side looked harsh and raw.

Laura went on talking. She spoke in generalisations, and then threw in casual remarks about cases she had had which bore out her generalisations. Charlotte, leaving the pain behind in the isolated farmhouse, was flattered, and tried to nod and look as though she understood what she was being told. Then she realised that there was no need for this. Laura was not anxious to communicate anything to her. Personal feelings and relationships did not come into it: Laura was thinking aloud, and Charlotte was merely someone receptive, someone to talk at.

Had she, Charlotte wondered, any personal feelings at all, except where Peter was concerned?

They approached the sea. The wind freshened, and thumped against the windows of the car. The road was running alongside a river, which met the sea near a cluster of buildings and slanting masts.

'Tapton Harbour,' said Laura, breaking off some long story and then omitting to take it up again.

They were close to the ranges now. While Laura drove off along a narrowing road to some scattered houses below the sea wall, Charlotte got out and walked to the river bank. On the farther bank, above the mud which glinted like fishes' scales, was a tall wire fence with a gate in it. A notice said something about ranges, firing, and a red flag flying: the remaining words were too small for her to read from this distance. Some way off along the shore, a spindly tower rose some forty feet into the air. Beyond that again, so far away that they looked like boxes littering the shingle, were rows of huts.

It was cold. Charlotte moved into the shelter of a public house which stood a little way back from the water's edge. Inside there was a murmur of voices, broken by an occasional laugh. She thought of going in. But she was not used to entering a pub alone. It was one of her quirks that had always amused Peter. She would never meet him in a pub, not even the most respectable sort. He used to laugh at her about that.

Two soldiers came through the gate on the other side. One of them stood by a wooden post and hammered a bell with a beater that hung beside it. Someone inside the pub cursed. The soldier hammered again. A man in a dirty blue jersey, and trousers that were tucked into piratical knee-boots, came out of the bar, stumped across to the bank, and disappeared over the edge.

Charlotte watched without curiosity. In this bleak landscape, one watched anything that moved. She felt quite detached. If Laura had come back at this moment and started up the car, Charlotte would have got in and let herself be driven somewhere else, and would have seen perhaps another village or a farmhouse, and none of it would have meant anything at all.

She watched as a rowing-boat appeared from under the shelter of the harbour wall and made its way across the narrow stretch of water. The two soldiers clambered in and were rowed over. In a few moments they appeared above the bank on this side.

Followed by the ferryman, they walked towards the pub.

One of them noticed Charlotte. He said something to his companion, and they both stared at her. The one who had spoken pursed his lips in a soundless whistle.

And Charlotte was suddenly awake.

Suddenly, unexpectedly, she was herself again. Her hand went up automatically to her hair. She pulled her sweater down over her breasts, and looked remotely out to sea, smiling to herself.

Yet in some odd way she wished Laura would come back now so that they could drive off.

The soldier who had first noticed her hesitated. She heard his companion say: 'Come on.'

'All right, there's no hurry.'

'I'm going in, anyway.'

'You go in. I'm not stopping you.'

The ferryman also went inside. There was the faint tinkle of a cash register.

The soldier said: 'It's cold to be hanging about out here.'

Slowly she turned to look at him.

'All right, all right,' he said; 'I only said it was cold.'

'Yes, it is.'

'Waiting for someone?'

'A friend,' said Charlotte.

'Is he going to keep you long?'

'She's a doctor. She's seeing a patient.'

Charlotte turned away, but did not move off.

'Come and have a drink while you're waiting.'

She had been wanting to go in, but now that she had been asked by this stranger she was not so sure. He had a bright, impertinent face. He took it for granted, she could tell, that most young women would say yes to him. But she could also tell that if she said no he would shrug, grin, and walk inside. And Laura would come, and they would drive away.

She said: 'It's not a bad idea.'

Her sense of time had been restored. She was alive, and this was a real place instead of a dream scene. She wanted to celebrate, wanted to tell someone, because it was important; but the next best thing was just talking to someone — anyone, about anything.

'Come on, then. Time for a quick one.'

The buzz of conversation slackened as they entered the bar, and then was renewed. The soldier, swaggering slightly, laughably like a pouter pigeon, said:

'What's yours?'

'Half of bitter, please.'

'Really? If you'd like something else — a short — '

'I like drinking beer.'

'Good for you.'

He brought the tankards to a small table near the window. They raised them and drank. Charlotte sighed and leaned back. The soldier cleared his throat and, for the first time, looked shy.

He said: 'Er — I'm Walter.'

'I'm Mrs. Swanton.'

'Oh, are you.' He looked dubiously into his beer.

'Charlotte Swanton,' she said.

'I haven't seen you in these parts before.'

'I haven't been here long.'

'Oh, I see.'

There was a long silence. At last Walter cleared his throat again, after a quick and angry glance at his friend, who was standing at the bar, grinning.

He said: 'There's a Doctor Swanton not far from here. Woman doctor.'

'My sister-in-law.'

'She came down to the camp once.' His

tone warmed. She had talked to so many soldiers in her time, and recognised the quickening of interest in his voice — that earnestness that always came into their voices when they talked about their army life, the only true reality, the standard by which everything else was measured. 'Came down once,' he said with relish, 'when the M.O. was off sick. But the boys wouldn't wear it.'

'Wouldn't they?'

'Not a woman doctor, they wouldn't.'

It was nice, thought Charlotte comfortably. Nice to hear all the voices about her, rising and falling, all mixed up. She relaxed. Walter went on talking, and she nodded and smiled. The smell of the sea, faintly acrid with harbour mud, blew in through the open door.

She said idly: 'It's a long way from anywhere, on those ranges.'

'You're telling me,' said Walter with a grimace. 'In the winter! I tell you, in the winter!'

And then Laura was standing in the doorway.

She said: 'When you're ready.'

There was a hush. Charlotte stared for a moment, then finished her drink. She smiled at Walter, got up, and went out with Laura. They got into the car. Laura said nothing.

'It was so cold outside,' said Charlotte. They headed inland, and the church towers gyrated once more. Laura stared straight ahead and drove fast.

Slowing for a corner, she said: 'If you like that sort of company, you could always get a job in the canteen down at the camp.'

'You don't have to be horrid.'

'Oh, great heavens,' said Laura inconsequentially.

'I was just having a drink, that's all. Anyone would think — '

'I merely suggested that if you were bored, you could get a job in the canteen,' said Laura.

'I've never done anything like that,' said Charlotte stiffly. 'I've never in my life done a job of that sort.'

'No, I don't suppose you have.' They were approaching Brookchurch. Laura added: 'And perhaps it would be dangerous, anyway. We wouldn't want to have to report to Peter that you'd been blown up.'

'Blown up?' Charlotte laughed uncertainly.

'Wandering about on those ranges, you're liable to tread on unexploded shells. It has been known to happen.'

There was something vicious in Laura's manner. It was as though she could say more, and was on the verge of doing so. But they were nearly home.

As they turned into Church Street, Laura said: 'When will you be going to see Peter, or don't you know yet?'

'I . . . I haven't thought about it.'

'Haven't you?'

'I don't know that I want to. I don't think I could bear it. You know I didn't go to the . . . the trial.'

'If he asks for a visit from you — '

'He won't. I'm sure he won't. I know Peter.'

Laura's lips tightened. But now they were home, and nothing else was said.

Charlotte felt different, and knew that Laura had noticed the difference. Laura was, in some indefinable way, aware of her as a person again, as she had been aware when they first met. The early days of Charlotte's stay here had been a lull. It was as though — the thought was absurd — the two of them were preparing for a struggle, and Laura had been coldly, correctly allowing her opponent to recover from an illness before attacking.

I can always go back to town, thought Charlotte. I can go back. I don't have to stay here, in this sort of atmosphere.

She could go back whenever she chose.

But she stayed. She stayed because the household routine here was so smooth; it provided her with a pattern for her days — a pattern which she knew only too well would be lacking once she returned to London. It was easier to put off such a decision; easier to stay than to go.

After all, Laura couldn't do her any harm. Laura didn't like her, but that was just unfortunate.

It wasn't as though Laura could do anything dreadful.

7

The telephone rang. There was only one shrill note before Laura had reached out and lifted the receiver.

'Is that Doctor Swanton?'

'It is.'

'It's the school here, Doctor. The grammar school.'

'Hello, Miss Jones. What is it this time — falling off the wallbars, broken legs, a split head . . . ?'

'A nasty bang on the arm. It's swollen up horribly. One of your patients.'

'Which one?'

'Gilbert Drysdale.'

Laura gave a slight start. She glanced at her watch.

'Gilbert Drysdale,' repeated the voice in the receiver.

'I'll be over right away.'

'Sorry to bring you all this way, but he *is* one of your patients.'

'Quite,' said Laura, knowing the inflection

and seeing in her mind's eye the headmaster of the school smirking his approval beside Miss Jones. 'I'm starting at once.'

She drove in towards the hills, and in ten minutes was drawing up outside the large school on the outskirts of Jury. Girls were singing loudly and inaccurately in one of the upper rooms. As she opened the front door and went in, the thump of feet from the gymnasium resounded along the corridor.

The headmaster had evidently been watching for her from his study window. He came out into the corridor, twitching his gown and bowing slightly.

'I'm so glad you could come, Doctor Swanton. It must be a nuisance for you to have to come all this way.'

'No nuisance at all,' said Laura curtly. 'Where is he?'

'In the headmaster's study,' said Mr. Cartwright impressively. He always referred to himself in the third person: the effect was one of detached admiration. 'The headmaster's study is not always the quietest place in the school' — he allowed a suitable interval for Laura to smile, then smiled himself — 'but in the absence of a sick bay it is not too dreadfully inadequate.' He held the door open and followed Laura in. 'There's little enough space for our new entry this coming year, without building sick bays and heaven only knows what else. I think people fuss too much these days. They would rather have canteens and clinics than classrooms.'

Gilbert Drysdale was sitting in an armchair with his left elbow resting on the arm. His narrow face was white, but he did not protest when Laura probed his arm with careful fingers.

Mr. Cartwright stood over them, watching with a distant, tolerant smile.

He said: 'I remember that once I broke two fingers on my right hand. I didn't say a word about it. Not a word. Boys in those days didn't make a fuss about trifles. I went to school as though nothing had happened.'

'A very stupid thing to do,' said Laura, without looking up.

Mr. Cartwright giggled. 'Well,' he said, 'how bad is this young man's injury?'

He bent down from his great height

over the boy in the chair, curling like a question mark. His face might have been considered ascetic but for the wide, restless eyes.

'He won't come to any harm,' said Laura. She took bandages from her bag. 'I'll immobilise his arm. He should be allowed to sit somewhere where he won't get bumped into. He won't be able to use his arm properly for a few days, but provided he isn't pushed about he'll make a quick recovery.'

'Splendid.' Mr. Cartwright unfolded, and was incongruously jovial from the heights of his six-foot-two slenderness. 'This'll give you an excuse for doing nothing, hm, young fellow?'

'Come to my surgery this evening between six and seven,' Laura told the boy. 'I'll have another look then.'

He got up and went to the door, which Mr. Cartwright opened with a flourish, aimlessly patting him on the shoulder as he went out.

Laura had very little time for Mr. Cartwright. He was too predictable. You knew what his next remark was likely to be, and you could usually deduce what odd, twisted schemes he was brewing up. He would, for example, not miss the present opportunity of making some reference to the nearness of the Jury doctor and to Laura's remoteness.

'Well, thank you for coming all this way.' Here it came. 'Of course we could have got Doctor Whiting — it seems silly not to call him in, when he's so close — but I know how worried you folk are about etiquette. And about losing patients to another doctor, eh?' He gave a happy splutter.

She did not bother to reply, knowing that there was nothing which unsettled him more than to be ignored. She picked up her bag and made for the door.

'Well, thank you,' he said again, effusively. 'Thank you. I hope we don't have to — er — worry you again.'

He was plucking at her attention, feeling that the interview had not been satisfactorily concluded.

'The boy will be perfectly all right,' said Laura, to round off the affair.

This gave him a lead. With his hand on

the doorknob, he wagged his head, leaning confidentially towards her. There was a stale smell arising from his gown. He said in an undertone:

'Rather a difficult case, that boy.'

'Indeed?'

If the boy had been anyone else, Laura would not have waited. She would have made it clear that she wanted to get away, and Mr. Cartwright would have been left in his study deploring the haste and rudeness of doctors. But this was a question of Gilbert Drysdale. Despite her impatience, she waited. However much she might try to pretend that she was not interested in this result of what had happened so many years ago — even that she detested the boy — she had to learn anything there was to be said about him.

'You know the case, of course? Living with his grandfather — mother ran off with an American soldier, and heaven knows who the father — '

'Yes, I know the case,' said Laura brusquely.

'How people can be so callous about their children's welfare . . .' Mr. Cartwright sighed a painful sigh. 'And now the grand-father wants to take him away from school at the end of the summer term.'

'He'll be fifteen by then?' She was startled, knowing that it must be so yet hardly able to believe it.

'Of course the law is that they can leave school when they're fifteen,' said Mr. Cartwright crossly. 'But when a grammar school place is accepted for a child, it should be done so on the understanding that that child will remain at least until sixteen — and preferably to eighteen.'

'Mr. Drysdale wants his grandson to start work?'

'They're all the same. Really, they have no sense of responsibility whatever. I make it quite clear that if there are any financial difficulties, or problems at home, the headmaster is here to help.'

'And,' said Laura maliciously, 'they don't realise that it knocks points off your salary scale, do they? Perhaps if you were to put it to them . . . '

Mr. Cartwright's mouth opened pro-testingly. Then he allowed it to stretch into a reluctant smile.

'Now, now! What a suggestion. Really!'

'Perhaps when I see old Drysdale, I'll have a word with him. For the boy's sake,' said Laura.

She had not expected him to look pleased. His gratitude was forced. He liked the right thing to be done; he genuinely, in his own muddled way, liked parents and guardians to be persuaded to do what was best for their children; but he liked to do the persuading himself.

'If you have any influence with him, that would be most kind of you,' he dubiously said.

Laura went out and drove home.

She left the car at the front of the house and went briskly in through the waiting-room.

'Oh!' Charlotte, startled by the opening of the door behind her, jumped away from the table. Then she smiled ingratiatingly.

Laura said: 'What are you doing?'

It had started out as no more than an idle, conventional query. She was quite indifferent to the ways in which Charlotte filled in time. But before the words were out of her mouth they had been an accusation. She stared at the jumble of magazines on the table.

'I was sorting things out,' said Charlotte.

'Sorting them out?'

The usual neat piles of *Punch*, *The Tatler* and the women's magazines had been toppled together. A few torn covers flapped over the edge of the table. The mutilation was as immediate a challenge to Laura as the sight of torn flesh in an accident would have been. Things that were torn, messy, loose and untidy demanded immediate action.

She pushed past Charlotte and began to extract the more battered magazines. These she put aside on a chair, and restored the others to their original piles.

'I was only looking out a few things,' protested Charlotte, making an occasional dab at some shred of paper which Laura unfailingly twitched away before she could reach it.

Laura held up the outer pages of a woman's weekly paper. Its centre pages had been removed.

'There was an article I wanted to read,' said Charlotte.

'And you actually tore the pages out, just for that?'

'I wanted to keep it.'

'It wouldn't occur to you that somebody else might want to read it? One of the patients for whom I supply these things, for instance. Somebody might want to finish the short story which runs on to one of those pages.'

Charlotte gave an abrupt, shrill laugh. 'You sound just like Peter.'

Laura stood very still. 'Do I?'

'Like Peter *used* to, at first.' Charlotte waved towards the table. 'He was always carrying on at me, at first. If I left a book behind a cushion, he'd feel it. Like the princess and the pea. He couldn't bear to see a book left open — face down, or anything like that — or anything with a coupon cut out of it, or a page torn.' She laughed again, this time wistfully. 'He was so silly.'

Laura took up the torn copies under her arm and turned towards the passage.

Charlotte, trying to assist and finding herself once more thwarted, said in an unsteady voice:

'He got it from you. All that sort of thing, it all came from you. But he grew out of it.'

'Did he?'

'He used to tell me about you,' Charlotte persisted, following Laura down the passage, raising her voice. 'We used to laugh about things like that.'

'Did you?'

'He used to thank me. He used to laugh, and thank me for . . . for saving him from being an old maid.'

Peter's mine, she was saying. Peter, she was assuring Laura, doesn't belong to you any more. I took him over, laughed at him, laughed with him, taught him to laugh at everything you shared; I own him now, you're nothing to him, we both laughed and we'll go on laughing and there's nothing of Peter left down here with you any more, nothing left, nothing . . .

Then Charlotte caught up with Laura and seized her arm. Laura jerked away from the contact.

'I'm only joking,' said Charlotte. 'It wasn't like that at all.'

'No?'

'Of course it wasn't. You know that. I'm only pulling your leg.'

'Are you? I see.'

Suddenly Laura knew what she intended to do. She could not have explained even to herself why she knew so surely that this was essential — could not have said what she hoped or expected from it. The plan rose within her, compelling, a devouring force, not to be denied.

She said: 'Would you like to help me this evening, Charlotte?'

'Help you?'

They were in the kitchen. Laura put the bundle of magazines down near the back door, and turned to face Charlotte. Mrs. Swanton watched them.

'You could give me a hand with evening surgery,' said Laura. 'I sometimes get quite a crowd here, you know, and it's difficult to cope with them all. If you could get all their names in the right order, and usher them in and out, and perhaps get their record cards out for me, it would make such a difference.'

Her mother stared at her disconcertingly.

'Whatever's got into you, Laura? You know you've always said you couldn't bear anyone else playing about with — '

'Things have been piling up just lately,' said Laura smoothly and untruthfully. 'Besides, it might give Charlotte a . . . well, let's call it an interest in life.'

Charlotte stuck out her lower lip and looked sullen. But she said: 'I think it would be interesting.'

'You can wear one of my white lab coats. You should look rather fetching.'

Charlotte's suspiciousness did not abate, but within the space of a few minutes there was a contemplative, anticipatory gleam in her eye. It was not hard to guess what her thoughts were; not hard for Laura, who felt that she was getting to know Charlotte very well — getting to know and despise her more and more. Charlotte was seeing herself as a trim, efficient receptionist. She would smile professionally, give a proprietorial glance at the rows of bottles in the consulting-room as she ushered a patient in, nod graciously when showing one out, and in a few weeks' time begin to make knowledgeable judgments of patients and their ailments.

Not that Laura had any settled intention of employing Charlotte regularly. She was merely experimenting, with particular concern for this evening. The first performance might well be the last. Charlotte herself would probably not want to go on after this evening.

8

Evening surgery was not, as it happened, a crowded one.

'You can get used to things gradually,' said Laura. 'Take your time.'

'I must try and do a lot more for you,' said Charlotte. She was eager and in some way remorseful. 'I've really been dreadfully idle. You must *make* me do things for you, Laura.'

The door outside closed quietly, and she hurried out.

Laura listened to the irregular opening and closing of the door, wondering when Gilbert Drysdale would come in. That shuffling step she recognised as old Cobbett's. The rachitic cough was Johnson's. That quiet opening and closing . . . that might be anybody.

Charlotte ushered them in and out with a smug little grin that at times threatened to get out of control. How she loved the whole business: it was pitiful. Really, a more vapid, thoroughly unsuitable wife for the erratic Peter it would have been hard to imagine.

Then, after a short spell of what Laura referred to as a brisk trade, culminating in a Bell's palsy case, there was a lull. Laura half rose from her chair, then decided to wait. She must not spoil the effect.

Once again the sound of the door. A pause, and Charlotte came in.

Her face had changed. She was pale and her lower lip seemed to have sagged. She looked helplessly at Laura.

Laura said: 'Who's next?'

'A boy. Gilbert Drysdale.' The name was barely audible.

'Oh, yes,' Laura casually said. 'Wheel him in.'

Gilbert came in, slouching slightly. He hesitated inside the door and glanced doubtfully at the glass case of surgical instruments in the corner.

'Well, and how's the elbow?' asked Laura.

Charlotte remained where she was for a moment, staring at the boy's face; then with the faintest noise in her throat she turned and went out.

Laura prodded the arm. The swelling had gone down. She nodded. 'Cleared up nicely. That didn't take long, did it?'

'No, miss,' said Gilbert with relief.

Already he was moving tentatively off the edge of his chair.

'But go easy with it for a little while.'

'Yes, miss.'

Laura said: 'Just a moment.'

He stopped, apprehensive.

'I've been wondering,' she said, feeling her way, 'if you'd like to earn some extra pocket money.'

He waited for her to go on.

'You have to cycle through Brook-church every evening on your way home from school — '

' 'Cept when I get the bus.'

'Yes. But the bus stops here anyway, so that needn't affect what I'm thinking of.' She took the cap off her pen and began to draw neat little diagrams on a prescription pad. Laura was not a confirmed doodler. When she did indulge herself, the results were invariably trim and formal. 'I thought,' she said, 'that you might be able to drop in here each evening to do a few odd jobs for me. My mother finds it hard to get about as freely as she would like, and there are all sorts of things she isn't fit to tackle. Chopping wood for starting the boiler — getting anthracite up from the shed — and I always have a batch of medicines to be taken down to the bus-stop. Usually they have to wait until morning: it would be a help if you could get them down in the late afternoon when you leave. You might even deliver a few of them to the actual addresses if they're on your way.'

Gilbert stared fixedly at a shelf ahead of him. He appeared both resentful and interested. He was at an age when accepting or discussing money no longer came easily; an age when he had uncomfortable intimations of a dignity which must be preserved.

Laura added: 'You could have something to eat here, and a cup of tea, to keep you going.'

'Oh, that . . . ' Gilbert waved the irrelevance aside.

'Perhaps you'd like me to have a word

with your grandfather?'

'I can do that myself, thank you, miss.'

'And you'll do it?'

'I'll have to see,' said Gilbert. He smiled tantalisingly, in a way that stabbed at her. 'I'll let you know, shall I?'

'Please,' said Laura.

'It'll be all right, anyway.' Gilbert finally got up.

It was as good as settled. She had done it, and had not even attempted to estimate the consequences. She saw it only as a situation rich in potentialities; she had only the vaguest idea of what the outcome could possibly be.

She sat there after Gilbert had gone, surprised and for a moment a little alarmed by her own impulsiveness. It was disturbing, the effect Charlotte had on her. But the alarm was momentary. What she was doing was in a way like trying a certain course of treatment on a patient. You thought your diagnosis was right, but the patient's description of symptoms was so vague that you could not yet be sure. You experimented cautiously . . . and usually you were right. It was gratifying to find how often you were right.

Only in this case she was really being very far from cautious.

She was still sitting there when Charlotte came in.

Charlotte stood in the doorway, and looked at her, and said:

'Why did you do that?'

'What's wrong, Charlotte?'

'That boy — you knew he was coming tonight, you knew, didn't you? That's why you asked me . . . You wanted me to see him.'

Laura said nothing.

'He's . . . he's Peter's son, isn't he?' said Charlotte.

Laura screwed the cap carefully back on her pen. It had worked, then. Yet now she realised that she had not expected recognition to be so instantaneous. A slight suspicion, perhaps: a disquiet that Charlotte would not be able to explain; and then, gradually, the dawning awareness. That was how it should have been. Not this sudden flash of intuition. Nobody else in the district, so far as she knew, was aware of the identity of Gilbert's father. Nobody else had noticed any resemblance — and the Brookchurch folk were, as a rule, maliciously observant.

Abruptly she was caught up in a great wave of jealousy. She was quite unprepared for it. The satisfaction she had hoped to win from revealing Gilbert to Charlotte had somehow turned sour. Instead, she felt this bitter loathing, this jealousy of a woman who was so stupid and so worthless and yet so much in love with Peter, so much a part of Peter, that she could tell at once who Gilbert was.

'Peter's son, isn't he?' Charlotte insisted.

Laura got up suddenly and began to replace record cards in their drawer. She said:

'Yes, he is.'

9

Peter wrote on drab paper the information that he had been moved to a prison in the North. It was one of the 'progressive' prisons, and he had no complaints. He did not want Charlotte to come and see him. He would sooner serve out his sentence alone, undisturbed. When he was free and could hold up his head again, they would meet and everything would be different.

Charlotte cried over the letter, and then felt hurt about it. He didn't want to see her. It was one of his poses, of course. The phrases had a familiar melodramatic ring about them. A month from now he might well be begging her to visit him.

When her immediate annoyance had died down, she admitted to herself that she was glad he did not want her to travel all that way. She was not sure that she could have faced him right now. She needed time; needed to get over the shock of this recent revelation. If she had made the long and doubtless exasperating journey now, she would have spent the hours in the train framing reproaches. She would have been keyed-up when she arrived, they would have quarrelled, and the journey back would have been wretched.

Better to wait. Better not to see him.

She would have liked to show the letter to Laura and to say, 'I told you he'd feel like this.' But she could not talk about Peter to Laura. Not yet. And under Laura's cold eyes the words would have spelled out only one thing, without other meanings or reservations: 'He doesn't want to see you. He's been thinking things over, and he doesn't want to see you.'

10

'I don't see why,' said Mr. Drysdale shortly. 'I jes' don't see why, that's all.'

He was a bulbous-featured man with a large nose. His skin was hard and wrinkled, like that of a gypsy or a sailor. He had worked for years in the open, chopping wood, making hurdles, splitting firewood, always slicing and hacking efficiently at something. When he spoke he used words as he would have used an axe: he smacked them down decisively, sure of his aim, as though there could never be any argument about anything he might choose to say. Gilbert was used to this, and did not make the mistake of supposing that such remarks were actually to be taken as final.

'She's managed all these years,' he went on, although Gilbert had not yet responded to his first protest. 'Why does she want to have you over there now?'

'She says Mrs. Swanton's getting past it.'

'Rubbish. Reck'n Bella's as sound as I am. Sounder, maybe. Same age. Her and your grandma went to school together. And if your grandma was alive today, she'd be hale and hearty enough. Of course, Bella always did have it easy . . . '
He snorted, then said: 'Well, what's it to be? I suppose there'll be no peace if you don't go.'

'I wouldn't mind,' said Gilbert.

'You may as well go. Though she won't have you for long, mind, with you at work soon after you break up in the summer.'

So it was settled. Gilbert began to call in at the doctor's house every evening on his way home. He emptied the bins in the consulting-room, filled the stove, and replenished the anthracite supply. He loaded wrapped and sealed medicines into his saddle-bag, and delivered them to the general store near the bus-stop, or called with them at some of the houses on his way home across the marsh.

His manner remained non-committal, but he was in fact enjoying himself. It meant a lot to him to be able to walk possessively into the consulting-room whether there was anyone there or not, where before he had been allowed in only when it was his turn as a patient. He liked the smell of the place and he liked the cool, damp silence of the waiting-room when there was nobody there.

Also he liked routine. His grandfather claimed to be an exact, tidy man, and other people believed the claim. They admired the way he looked after Gilbert. He certainly did his best; but he was not really at ease indoors. He tried very hard. But Doctor Swanton, Gilbert found, had everything just the way she wanted it without having to try. Or so it seemed.

Gil found himself working to a time-table, and enjoyed it. He enjoyed, too, the way Mrs. Swanton fussed over him, always pressing him to have another slice of cake at tea, and watching him anxiously as he worked.

'Don't try to lift too much, Gil,' she would say as he carried a bin out. 'Really we could do with a man . . . but with Mrs. Emery coming in to do the cleaning, really there's so little . . . ' And when he was chopping sticks she would peer into the shed and cluck: 'Do mind your fingers. I'm always so afraid . . . '

He liked Mrs. Swanton, and often wondered about her. He could not imagine her as a girl at school with his grandmother. He remembered his grandmother only dimly, as someone old and gnarled like his grandfather — and Mrs. Swanton just didn't fit in with somebody like that.

Doctor Swanton, too, was all right. In a different way, of course. She was a bit severe, but when she wanted a job doing she said so straight out, and you understood right away what she was after. She was what made the house go: he thought of this house as *going*, always in motion, like a bus that had to carry people from one place to another, with a proper schedule. It was all organised so that surgery should start at six o'clock. By then he had left; but he was governed by the approach of surgery time, and it took on an imposing, almost religious quality for him. His own home was full of his grandfather's memories and a smell of the past. His own home had slowed down and nearly stopped ages ago.

There was only one thing in the doctor's house that was not quite right; one thing that didn't match up.

That was Mrs. Swanton — the other Mrs. Swanton, the one they called Charlotte. She didn't belong at all. You never knew where she would be. Her day was not mapped out for her as it was for the others. Sometimes she would be walking down the road as Gil cycled up, sometimes leaning from a window. Often he did not see her at all. Indoors, she might pop up anywhere, at any time, but she never seemed to be doing anything special.

Any time they passed she looked at him so queerly. He couldn't make it out. She was queer, all right.

In the middle of his second week, his grandfather asked him how he was getting on. He fired off the question, just as he had fired it off once before, on Gil's first day there, as though waiting to pounce on whatever he said.

Gil shrugged. 'All right,' he said. He would not have dreamed of telling his grandfather how much he liked the place: he knew, without thinking it out in any detail, how he would have snorted and made some remark about 'getting high and mighty if we don't watch out, I can see' . . . and how, ridiculously, he would have been hurt by praise of someone else's house.

'What's Bella like these days?'

'She's all right,' he said.

Mr. Drysdale sighed. 'That all you can say?' He tried again: 'The doctor's kept pretty busy, so I'm told.'

'In and out all the time,' Gil agreed. Then he added: 'The other one's a bit funny.'

'Which other one?'

'The one they call Charlotte.'

'They got a girl workin' for 'em too?'

'No. Her proper name's Mrs. Swanton too. At least, that's what the doctor said when she introduced me. I haven't spoken to her much since.'

'Mrs. Swanton? Now who could that be?' The old man had been sawing slices off a sandwich loaf. He stopped and pointed the knife at a point beyond Gil's shoulder. 'Swanton's a common enough name in these parts, Lord knows, but I never heard tell of *them* bein' related to any of the others.' The knife became fixed and accusing. 'There's never been only but the one boy. And you don't mean to tell me . . . ' He took a deep breath. 'Well, I never. If I'd knowed that,' he said angrily; 'if I'd knowed that, before you went there . . . '

'What's up?'

'Nothing. Least said soonest mended.'

He could pack such condemnation into a banal remark. His voice gave Gil a queer feeling. There was something odd about the one they called Charlotte, no doubt about it.

The next time the two of them met, he was raking out the boiler. He had his head up through the trap door in the floor of the passage, and there she was, coming into the kitchen from the garden. She wasn't carrying an armful of washing, or a bucket, looking busy — not even any flowers or anything: she was just on the wander, like she always was.

He drew the bucket of ash up and put

it outside, away from the flap, and then climbed out into the passage.

'All right, miss, won't be a minute.'

She blinked as she came in. He let the flap down and moved the bucket out of her way.

'Thank you,' she said, her lips hardly moving.

'Dangerous, this thing,' said Gil. 'Coming in out of the light, you could easy go straight down in.'

'Yes,' she said. 'Yes, it is.' Then her face seemed, even in that uncertain light, to flush. She went past, and he heard her going upstairs.

He picked up the bucket. For a moment he stood on the spot she had walked over. She had left a sweet, fading scent behind her. Doctor Swanton didn't use scent like that. And, of course, Doctor Swanton didn't wear clothes like hers.

He thought, for the first time, how pretty Mrs. Swanton — Charlotte — was.

11

Charlotte had waited a long time before speaking. She could not, simply would not ask Laura any questions. That would have been too much: that would have been doing what Laura wanted.

They hardly exchanged a word nowadays save on professional matters. For Charlotte had gone on acting as receptionist. Stubbornly, because Laura had so clearly expected that she would want to give it up, Charlotte had carried on with the job. She had not asked Laura whether she wished her to do so or not: she had simply appeared to take it for granted. It was up to Laura to tell her to stop. Almost it was as though she had thrown down the challenge to Laura.

Laura would not speak.

All the while, Charlotte was hugging her terrible curiosity to herself. She endured it for as long as she could, and then blurted out to Mrs. Swanton:

'That boy, Gilbert, who comes here — who's his mother?'

'Nobody you'd know,' said Mrs. Swanton unhappily.

'Not yet, anyway.'

'What makes you ask?'

'Because it's so obvious,' said Charlotte, 'who his father is.'

'I don't understand, dear.' Mrs. Swanton was making a gallant effort.

Charlotte said: 'You needn't bother to cover it up. Laura's already admitted it.'

'Oh, she hasn't! Oh, how could she . . . '

'I knew right away.'

Mrs. Swanton shuffled fussily towards the kitchen table and subsided into a chair. She stared at a cabbage that had just been delivered, peeled off one of the outer leaves, and then shook her head.

'What a shame. But' — she summoned a hopeful smile — 'it's all over now. There's nothing to worry about.'

There was something remarkably soothing and convincing in the way she said it. There, Charlotte had to accept, nothing to worry about. Not that she had really been worrying: it was just that she had seemed, when she first saw that boy's face, to be robbed of breath, and the breath was only now coming back.

She said: 'I'd like to . . . to hear about it, though. To know. Where the girl is, and — '

'Oh, goodness knows where she's got to by this time.'

'She didn't . . . doesn't look after him, then? She isn't in the district?'

'Not that young woman. It wasn't gay enough round these parts for her. She ran off when Gilbert was only little. Ran off with an American during the war.'

'To America?'

'I shouldn't think so. No, I don't think she'd get that far. I expect she got tired, or *he* got tired, before very long. There wasn't much to her.'

There wasn't much to her . . .

Charlotte faltered. 'But Peter — '

'He was only a boy. She must have put ideas into his head. We never discovered how it all started' — Mrs. Swanton was hastening to get this over and done with, talking with hurried emphasis as though to convince herself as well as Charlotte — 'but you may be sure it was that girl.'

'She was pretty?'

'You might say she was pretty. Very forward. A real little hussy. Yes,' said Mrs. Swanton firmly and judicially, 'she was pretty.'

There were so many questions that clamoured for an answer. Most of them would never be answered, for they were too intimate or too searching or there was nobody here capable of being truthful about them.

She ventured: 'Peter didn't want to marry her?'

'He most certainly did not.' Mrs. Swanton became almost indignant. 'There were plenty of them who'd have liked to catch him, but he was far too wily. It would have taken a smart girl to catch Peter.'

It was hard to tell whether she spoke affectionately or disapprovingly of her son. All deep emotion seemed to have been abandoned years ago beneath that pleasant, unvarying surface chatter. Only minor worries disturbed that surface — the sort of mild perturbation that flickered over her plump features now, as she realised what she had said.

'Oh, what a thing to say! I didn't mean . . . '

Charlotte laughed with her, evenly and politely. 'I'm sure you didn't.'

'And there's really nothing you need concern yourself with,' Mrs. Swanton went on, coming up with determination for the last sprint. 'What's done is done. You needn't hold it against the boy. It wasn't his fault.'

'Does Gil know about it?' asked Charlotte.

'Heavens, no. He's been told his father was killed in an accident, and his mother went off to hospital and died when he was little.'

'I'd have thought the girl — the mother — would have made some sort of fuss.'

'It was made worth her while not to,' said Mrs. Swanton, resenting this prolongation of a distasteful topic.

'Who made it worth her while?'

'We did. That is, Laura did. That is,

Reginald — my husband — did at first, so that Peter's career shouldn't be ruined. And when he passed on, Laura went on giving money regularly to make sure the child didn't suffer. Old Drysdale gets it — it's pretty well all that keeps the two of them going nowadays.'

'But Peter — Peter could have — '

'Laura would never have him worried,' said Mrs. Swanton. 'You know what she is.'

Yes, thought Charlotte. And then: No. Did she know what Laura was?

'It was all over years ago,' said Mrs. Swanton beseechingly. 'It's over, and that's that. You don't even have to think about it.'

'No,' said Charlotte.

She didn't even have to think about it. No point in bearing grudges against some young girl who had seduced, or been seduced by, Peter. The Peter of those days had, in any case, been left behind. To Charlotte he was a complete stranger: *her* Peter was a different person, with no ties to claim him from the past. She had never made any querulous claims on him, never demanded information or excuses.

Or, at any rate, not often.

This youthful silliness must be accepted and then not thought about any more.

It was a pity that Gilbert's face should be there to remind her so clearly — to remind her of Peter, and Peter's folly, and how much Peter owed to Laura.

The thought of the bond between Peter and Laura was the most frightening thought of all. She felt menaced by it.

'Well, that's cleared the air,' said Mrs. Swanton unexpectedly. She got up, and came and kissed Charlotte. 'Hasn't it?'

'Yes,' said Charlotte. 'Oh, yes.'

12

The wind was against him this afternoon. Tomorrow there would probably be rain, and he might have to come to school by bus. He put his head down, and pedalled grimly. The grasses by the roadside bent over in the direction from which he had come.

A hundred yards outside Brookchurch he was so puffed that he had to stop and lean against the wall of the small bridge. Even the sheltered water below was twitched from time to time by feathery ripples.

A path following the bank of this ditch led to a farmhouse a short distance away. Gil watched a woman coming along the path with a basket. It was not until she came closer that he really looked intently at her and saw that it was Charlotte.

The wind whipped her skirt and her hair sideways. He saw that she was laughing into the wind, not seeing him;

just laughing at the wind. He knew how she felt. You only had to part your lips slightly and you could hear and feel the air rushing in, singing between your teeth.

It was not until she reached the road that she saw him. She faltered, then came on, and nodded to him.

'Hello, miss . . . er, Mrs. Swanton,' he said.

'Hello . . . ' She hesitated, but did not use his name. 'On your way to do the chores?'

'That's it,' he said.

She looked along the road to the house. He could have pushed himself away from the wall with his left foot and cycled away — she was half expecting him to — but he did not. He got off his bike and stood on the far side of it from her. They began to walk along together.

She said: 'I've just been for some eggs from the farm.'

'Duckett's,' he said.

The wind whipped the name from his mouth and twisted it. She said: 'No, I'm not fond of duck eggs myself.'

'No.' He laughed more loudly than was

really necessary. 'No, I mean Duckett's is the name of the farm.'

'Of course it is.' She laughed again into the wind; they were both smiling. Then she said: 'Do you like school?'

It was the obvious ordinary silly question that so many folk asked, and was usually worth no more than a grunt of vague assent or an awkward laugh. But today Gil found himself answering seriously:

'It's all right. I mean, I like some of the masters. Miss Holyoake isn't so good.'

'You don't like women teachers?'

'Oh, I don't know.' He was careful, afraid that any remark about women teachers might seem to include women in general and therefore herself. 'They're all right, I suppose.'

'Of course, you've got girls in your school as well.'

'Yes,' he grunted.

Hair blew into her eyes. She pushed it back, and there was something lovely about the way she moved. He looked at her and looked quickly away.

She asked: 'Have you got a girl friend there?'

That was something she oughtn't to have asked. It was the one silly, awful question you didn't forgive. Of course there was Johnson, you had to admit there were blokes like Johnson — and Wright, W.E., messed about with girls in the Lower Sixth. There was a lot of talk about those two and those two girls during the lunch hour out on Denge's field. But what you would talk about with other members of the Fifth wasn't a thing you wanted to gas about outside. Inside, it was a joke; outside, it just made you go red.

'I oughtn't to have asked that,' said Charlotte. 'I'm sorry.'

In a way — he stole a surreptitious glance at her — she was like one of the girls at school. Like the only one Gil was at all interested in, and interested in her only because she was sensible. But even so, it was hard to imagine that girl Marion ever growing to look like this. Marion looked nice and cool and fresh sometimes; but sometimes he had seen her when she and the others came in damp and hot and streaky from P.T. or Games, and then she was awfully blotchy.

This Mrs. Swanton, now, was flushed by the wind, but not blotchy.

She said: 'I wish I knew more about the flowers and birds and all the rest of it.' Then she giggled. 'I meant on the marsh, of course.'

He could not see why she had thought the remark was funny. Of course she had meant on the marsh; he had understood right away that that was what she must mean. But he had noticed that she had these odd fits of laughter that didn't make sense.

'Do you know a lot about them?' she asked, looking at him sideways with an eagerness that was not just the usual grown-up eagerness to look interested. Too interested they looked as a rule, and you knew they were putting it on.

'A bit,' he said.

They reached the house, and she held the gate open while he wheeled his bike in.

'You must tell me all about it one day,' she said.

'Yes,' he said, a bit disappointed, because that was the sort of remark you didn't believe in: you could bet nothing would come of it, and nothing was ever meant to come of it.

He was wrong. It was hard to tell whether Charlotte and he met by accident or whether she arranged to be about when he went in a certain direction. What was certain was that their paths crossed far more frequently than they had done hitherto. Charlotte would stop and have a word with him in the house; she would be downstairs while he was having his cup of tea and slice of cake; she, like the older Mrs. Swanton, was now telling him not to try to carry too many things at once and not to overwork himself chopping sticks.

Always she had that queer thoughtful look on her face. And Doctor Swanton, too: *she* had a way of watching when she came across the two of them together that was funny, as though she couldn't make up her mind about something she was going to do or going not to do.

None of this worried Gil. He was used to being watched: from his earliest days he had been conscious of his grandfather's sharp, attentive face turned towards him. The heavy face and the shrewd, querulous eyes, always keeping him under observation. It had not bothered him. He had taken it all for granted — it was something adult, something the old fusspots couldn't help doing — and now he took for granted the way the Swanton women hovered over him.

One Friday evening Charlotte (Mrs. Swanton he called her to her face, and would have called her when speaking of her to the others if he had ever spoken of her to the others, which he hadn't) said:

'I'll walk a little way along the road with you, Gil. I could do with a breath of fresh air before surgery.'

Her 'before surgery' came out as crisply and professionally as though it were Doctor Swanton herself speaking.

They walked slowly. Today there was the usual marsh breeze, muttering along the ground. Charlotte glanced up at the telegraph wires.

'Look!' she cried. 'Those birds. Just like notes of music on a stave, aren't they? I wonder what the tune would be if you could whistle it?'

Gil looked up dubiously, and said nothing.

'Don't *you* think it looks like music?' she said enthusiastically.

He was suddenly frank. He said: 'No. They're just swallows.'

She raised her eyebrows, and pouted. Her whole face twisted in exaggerated surprise. Then she laughed. 'You're very literal, aren't you?'

'Well . . . ' he muttered.

He found that she was always doing that sort of thing. Whenever she saw anything she wanted to turn it into something else. Everything was 'like' something else. He didn't see the sense of it. But when, a few days later, the English master at school talked about similes, it came home to Gil more strongly than it had ever done just what a simile was. Not that that made it any better. He had always been sure that stuff was a lot of nonsense, and now he knew. But after that he went on looking for similes until it became a game he couldn't stop, like adding up the numbers on railway engines or motor cars and dividing them up and seeing if the last two figures added up to the same as the first two or could be divided into them or anything like that.

Charlotte asked a lot of questions. One or two vague ones about his mother that he couldn't make head or tail of. And what was he going to do when he left school? That was an old one, a dull and ordinary one that people were always asking, and it wasn't made any better by the fact that he didn't know what he was going to do. His grandfather had told him he was going to leave. His grandfather had said he would 'speak to someone' about him, get him 'fixed up'. Gil had no idea who that someone might be.

For himself, he wanted to go in for farming. He wanted to do it properly, and go to the big Agricultural College fifteen miles away: that was the only way to make a proper job of it, like Ted Noakes's older brother had done. But you had to stay on at school and take Advanced level in the G.C.E. for that, Mr. Cartwright had told him, and as he wasn't staying on, that settled that. He had to earn some money. His grandfather couldn't get about much nowadays after knocking himself on the leg, and his veins being bad anyway, so there would soon have to be some more money coming into the house.

It was better when Charlotte asked him about the plants that grew up out of the ditches. Then he could give her the answers without having to think them out and fret about them. It was funny how little she knew. She kept stopping him in the middle of a sentence and asking him to explain something that everyone understood.

But he liked her. He got to like her more and more while they went walking out of doors. She sounded interested in what he said, as though she really meant it. Although there were so many things she was ignorant about, she wasn't what you'd call silly.

He was glad that none of his school friends had so far seen him out with her: the things they'd have said would have been all wrong and would have spoilt the whole business. Yet at the same time he would have been proud, in a way, to be seen with her.

Indoors it was a bit different. He didn't think quite so much of her then. She showed up badly against the others. Doctor Swanton was tidy and liked everything just so, and she had made her mother fit in with her ways. But Charlotte wasn't tidy. Magazines left crumpled on chairs usually belonged to Charlotte, or had been taken by Charlotte from the waiting-room to read, and not returned. A bottle of cleansing lotion on the stairs, or a dropped handkerchief, would prove to be Charlotte's.

More than once Gil had seen Doctor Swanton stop, frown, and stoop to pick something up.

Once he saw her come downstairs and then hesitate, noticing, just as she was about to tread on it, a small perspex box filled with odds and ends. She paused. She had not seen Gil. Then, abruptly, she brought her foot down hard, and the box splintered.

A moment later she was saying to Charlotte: 'I'm sorry, but I've smashed something you left on the stairs.'

'Oh, my little box.'

'I'm afraid I don't expect to find things in the middle of the stairs. I just came right down on it.'

Still things were left lying around. Liking the orderliness of this house as he did, Gil was on the doctor's side; but he felt a bit uneasy about that one episode.

One afternoon he stayed somewhat later than usual. In a way he was hoping to be delayed: he wanted to walk out through the waiting-room just before surgery, past all the people sitting mournfully on chairs and waiting their turn.

Upstairs, Charlotte was thumping about. As usual she had left everything until the last minute, and had now decided to have a quick bath. Gil envied her. She showed people in and out. She looked very trim in her white coat — he had only once seen her wearing it, but the picture remained clear in his mind — and he had heard folk say how pleasant she was. 'A bit fussy, mind,' and, 'Gives herself airs — not a bit like the doctor,' but he wouldn't care what anyone said if he could be neat and efficient and perhaps make up medicines and in the end learn to be a doctor himself.

No, that was no good. You didn't get to be a doctor like that. The uneasy awareness came over him that he was nearing the end of his school life: if he had wanted to be a doctor probably he ought to have thought of it earlier.

Anyway, he didn't really fancy the idea, when he came to think about it. It was only something that moved him when he walked through this house, sniffing at the antiseptic smell by the consulting-room door, and seeing the doctor's bag on the ledge where she always dumped it when she came in.

Doctor Swanton appeared from the kitchen.

'Gilbert, will you run upstairs and fetch me a clean towel from the airing cupboard? Goodness knows what's happened to them all.'

'Yes, Doctor,' he snapped smartly. It sounded crisp and military when you rapped it out like that.

He went upstairs two at a time.

Charlotte's white lab coat was draped over the banister on the landing. One shoe projected into the corridor from a half-open door. He went towards the airing-cupboard, and at that moment the bathroom door was jerked open, and Charlotte came out.

She had a dressing-gown loosely over her shoulders. It hung lopsidedly, and fell away from her as she moved.

Gil stopped, appalled. He could not retreat. He saw her breasts and the shadows of her body, and the flash of her legs as they twitched back the trailing folds of the dressing-gown.

She gave a little squeal of laughter and hurried past him. The laugh echoed on in his head. There was a swirl of soapy perfume about him.

He found that he was breathing fast. He felt queer inside. Automatically he opened the door of the cupboard and took out a towel. When he had it, he did not at once go downstairs. He had to lean against the door for a minute. He was almost frightened of going back along the corridor, past Charlotte's door, which she had not closed properly.

'Gilbert!'

Doctor Swanton was at the foot of the stairs.

'Yes . . . coming.'

He went down, clutching the towel.

She looked at him curiously. 'Anything wrong?'

'No, miss. Nothing.' He took a deep breath. 'Here's your towel.'

'Thank you.'

Her eyes glanced past him, up towards the landing. The sweet, steamy, soapy smell leaked faintly down from the bathroom. The lab coat on the banister was suddenly tweaked away by an unseen hand.

'Well, it's about time you went home,' said Doctor Swanton in a hard, toneless voice.

'Yes. I'll be off.'

Of course she could not know, could not have guessed what had happened. If she did, it hadn't been his fault anyway. But there was something savage and accusing in her eyes. He hurried away, leaving her standing at the foot of the stairs, looking up, not even answering his 'Goodbye, Doctor.'

13

Laura took out her scissors and indicated to Mr. Drysdale that he should stretch his leg out. Then she began to cut down the adhesive bandage.

'Lot o' fuss,' said Mr. Drysdale ungratefully. 'Doctor Swanton would never ha' made all this fuss.'

Doctor Swanton was always, to him, Laura's father. She was just Laura — in his own mind, for he never addressed her by any name at all.

'Healed very well,' said Laura. She was surprised at the way the ulcer had cleared up in the past ten days. He was a tough, healthy old creature.

'Good job, too. Now I can get about properly again.'

'You'll still need your elastic stocking — '

'Oh, *them* things.'

He scowled down at his right leg as, though it did not belong to him. The skin was pink and puffy where it had been swathed in bandage. It made a bright contrast to his weather-beaten face and hands; and to the thick, knotted blue veins that twisted like grotesque cables up his leg.

Laura thought for a moment. The recovery had been remarkable, but in many ways that was going to make her task more difficult. She knew he would be furious at the suggestion she was going to have to make.

She began: 'You can't go on like this, Mr. Drysdale.'

'What's wrong now? You jus' said yourself it's healed up proper.'

'But the next time you go out and give yourself a bang on the leg — '

'It was an accident, that last one.' Mr. Drysdale was furious that he should be considered so inept. 'That's one thing that won't happen again, I lay.'

'Accidents happen whether you want them to or not. With your veins in their present condition, a hard knock against a chair could make another hole like that last one. Another ulcer — more bandages.'

She snapped the words out as brusquely as he himself might have done.

He answered in the same way. 'I'll keep me wits about me, thank you. It's high time I was doing something useful.'

'It's high time you were in hospital,' said Laura.

His mouth worked. He was trying to summon up some devastating remark that would put paid to all fancy notions of that sort. Finally he managed:

'Never heard of such a thing. Can't afford it, anyways.'

'Hospital treatment is free nowadays.'

'Can't afford the time,' he swiftly amended.

'If you go on as you have been doing, your veins will get worse. You're nearly crippled now — '

'No such thing.'

'You can't walk four miles up to the woods and do your work properly in your condition. The only treatment that will put you right is what they can do for you in hospital.'

'Well, I'm not going, and that's all there is to it.'

It was definite. There must be no

further argument. He clipped his words off with a little contemptuous expulsion of breath like a brief laugh. Nothing, said his face, could possibly make him change this decision.

It was all so familiar; all in keeping with the smug, exasperating, self-applauding local saying, 'We won't be druv.' The locals — the true locals, the older people who were still, in this modern world, a sullen tribe apart — would not only not be driven: they could hardly even be led, coaxed or cajoled.

'For your own good . . . ' began Laura, and then sighed.

They would not be told. Time after time she had been faced with this unreasoning stubbornness. Often she longed to leave such pig-headed folk to their fate. All right: let them have it their own way; let them see what happened when they disregarded her advice.

Of course she never, in the end, left matters like that. Always she persisted. Always her reluctant professional pride drove her on. She jeered at herself, but persevered.

Now she said: 'It's silly to be obstinate. They'll only keep you in for about three weeks.'

'Well, I'm just not goin' to — '

'In that time your veins can be tied and injected. It's safe and simple, and when you come out you'll be yourself again.'

'There's the boy,' said Mr. Drysdale with absolute finality. 'There's Gilbert. What about him, eh?'

Laura moistened her lips. What about Gilbert, indeed? She had not thought of him until now — and now she wished she did not have to. The challenge had been thrown suddenly across her path; she felt as though she had stumbled and were now lurching forward trying to regain her balance.

Mr. Drysdale glared triumphantly at her. 'What about him, eh? Couldn't go off and leave him on his own, specially with the Easter holidays comin' on. Who'd look after him, eh?'

Now she must back down. She could, and must, stop insisting. Already she was aware of danger — of what a stay in hospital would mean, not for Mr.

Drysdale but for herself. The implications assembled themselves in her mind.

But her professional integrity was as saving as a painful inoculation given many years ago, an inoculation which had not weakened but had somehow stiffened its resistance over the years.

She said: 'There's room for him at our place. We can look after him. It will only be for three weeks or so.'

No, said some part of her — that part of her which was not the doctor but Laura the woman, Peter's sister. No. This was unthinkable.

But she had spoken, and now would not draw back.

Mr. Drysdale had been taken quite off guard. He wriggled, and made dubious noises in his throat.

'Couldn't think of it,' he said at last. 'Very kind of you, but — '

'If you don't go into hospital now and get it over with,' said Laura firmly, 'you're going to be a nuisance to Gilbert in the future. He already does more than his share of the household . . . oh, yes he does' — as he tried to interrupt her

— 'and soon he'll have to devote his entire time to looking after you. There's no telling when you may be completely laid up: perhaps the very week he's starting his new job and needs to have no home worries to distract him.'

He was retreating. His eyes avoided hers. Once more he was staring with bitter enmity at his leg, which was betraying him so shamefully.

He said: 'I can't be beholden to you — '

'You know very well,' said Laura remorselessly, 'that we have certain responsibilities where Gilbert is concerned. We've done what we could — '

'You've always done what's right by him.'

'We want to continue. And I say that Gilbert must come to us now.'

'You agreed,' said Mr. Drysdale, making a last attempt, 'not to interfere. I was to have the say in what he did — in everything about the lad. That's the way we agreed it.'

'Yes,' said Laura. 'But in the present circumstances . . . '

133

He was defeated. From the moment she had committed herself to the decision that, all other considerations firmly set aside, he needed to go into hospital and *must* go into hospital, he had been defeated.

She had done what had to be done. The results of all this, like the results of Charlotte's arrival in Brookchurch, were hazy and far off; but somehow, somewhere, it was all going to add up, and there would be an answer.

14

Gilbert was given the small room at the end of the landing, overlooking the path by the side of the house. On very stormy days the wind would force rain through the window-frames, which in the course of many years had been reduced to the consistency of blotting-paper. For some reason the whole room smelt faintly of damp newspaper. But it was nevertheless, Laura knew, far better than Gilbert's room at home.

It was obvious that Gilbert was delighted by what had happened. He was startled by the efficiency with which breakfast was made — and, one felt, somewhat startled by his own efficiency in getting off to school on time. Mrs. Swanton made it her job to look after him: at first she treated him warily, as though never sure what he might say or do, but within a day or two she was bullying him amiably in a way she had never been able to adopt with Laura, who had coldly answered back, or with Peter, who had laughed brightly and ignored her.

On a Friday afternoon the school broke up for the Easter holiday.

The weather seemed promising. On Saturday morning the sky had that burnished appearance which it usually did not acquire until deep summer, and then not invariably. The freshness of the breeze kept it from being a hot day; but it was a day for walking across the marsh to the sea, and during lunch Gilbert looked continually out of the window.

'Going anywhere special this afternoon?' said Laura idly. She wondered, with that same sensation of feeling her way, whether now was the time to take him out in the car, casually, and begin talking to him, casually.

Charlotte looked up and said: 'Shall we go for a walk, Gil? There are lots of things I want to ask you about the dykes.'

Laura watched. The boy looked at Charlotte, and went faintly pink.

'All right,' he muttered. His voice was

reluctant, but that did not imply that he was reluctant to go out with her.

Laura had never been able to provoke that shyness in boys or men. Never. She had watched her school friends maturing, learning and practising; had watched the ease with which they brought on that awkwardness, and had scorned them for their cheap laughter and jubilation afterwards. She wouldn't have stooped to such nonsense. And if she had done, she could not have succeeded. She had always known that.

The sight of a grown woman exercising these powers on an adolescent was disgusting.

Charlotte and Gilbert went out together, and were away for some hours. Most of the time they were in full view of the back windows of the house — two distant specks in the bright haze of the marsh. Called out on one urgent visit that proved to be not at all urgent, Laura passed close to them late in the afternoon as she drove round the winding roads. They were bent over a ditch, and from this short distance it was clear that Gil was explaining something to Charlotte. His whole attitude was that of someone engrossed in a subject, sharing an enthusiasm.

Laura drove past them on her way out and on her return. They paid no attention to the car passing.

On Sunday morning, Charlotte announced that she and Gilbert were going to church.

'How nice,' said Mrs. Swanton. 'We'll all go.' Charlotte and Gilbert did not exactly exchange glances, but there was a slight movement of mutual commiseration.

'That'll be lovely,' said Charlotte.

She smiled uncertainly at Laura. Gilbert, too, looked at Laura. He wanted her approval. He might be fond of Charlotte, but he needed Laura's approval. She was glad of that. It would make things easier — those vague but important things that were not yet clearly formulated.

She said: 'Not for me. I remain a slave to the telephone.' And then she flicked out at Charlotte: 'I don't remember you bothering about church any other Sunday since you've been here.'

'We just thought it'd be nice. It's such a sweet little church.'

Gilbert had turned his attention to Charlotte's face. He heaved a sigh of relief when she had spoken, as though she had made everything all right. It was an addition to the routine — something else into which he gladly fitted once it had been sanctioned.

'I'd better not come, after all,' said Mrs. Swanton. 'The dinner . . . '

Laura could have offered to look after the dinner. Instead, she chose deliberately to let the two of them go alone. At the back of her mind lay the thought: Let them talk drivel to one another; let them think they're becoming friends; and then let's see what happens when . . .

When what?

She was not ready yet to give the answer.

'You don't mind' — thus Charlotte, on the Monday — 'if Gil and I go down to Tapton Harbour for the afternoon? I'll be back in time for surgery.'

'No need to worry about that. I managed before you came,' said Laura in a tone that could have been humorous but was not, 'and no doubt I'll manage later when . . . when you've gone.'

Alone at her desk, she thought about Peter. Instead of trying, as she had so often tried, to keep him at a distance, she invited him back into his home. She sat quite still, and heard his laughter, muffled, somewhere at the back of the house. A tune was whistled.

Peter.

The door would close with a click, and he would come in. Careless as he was, he never slammed doors. He had a mincing, affected way of leaning on a door and half swinging with it, letting the catch click home. On the rare occasions when he entered briskly, you knew he had done something wrong — very wrong.

She heard his voice as he explained. Always reasoning, explaining something away.

Then the voice faded. She half rose from her chair, as though if she hurried she might catch Peter on his way out through the waiting-room. But the sound had gone farther away than that: it fell into the tumultuous silence of the marsh, and was lost.

It would come back. When it did come back, she would not allow it to be confused and distorted by the overtones of other voices. Of Charlotte's voice.

She got up and went to the bench to tidy up record cards. After a minute or two she found herself surveying the bottles on the shelf immediately in front of her. There was nothing much here. But in the poison cupboard on her left there were so many things.

The thought took her unawares, and shocked her. She thrust it away. It went and sat on the edge of her mind, patiently waiting until she was ready to recall it.

15

She had, she admitted, thrown them together. But it had not been part of the plan — unsure as she was of its ramifications, Laura nevertheless knew that it could be no part of the plan — that Charlotte and Gilbert should get on so well. The sound of their confiding voices as they left the house, and their laughter in the spring afternoon, were not right.

But she was not perturbed. She noted with satisfaction that Gilbert continued to seek her approval. He might enjoy chattering to Charlotte, and in his gawky adolescent way perhaps he was absurdly infatuated with her; but she, Laura, was his standard of reference. Sometimes, even, he edged away from Charlotte when she was talking too loudly, with that exasperating intensity which she so often brought to bear on trivialities. In the sidewise glance of his eyes he disclaimed her.

I can get him if I want, thought Laura with a strange exultation. It was somehow important that she should be sure of this. He's mine, she thought, when I need him: I've only got to reach out and I can take him from her.

Just as, in due course, she would be able to take Peter from her. Or take her from Peter. Laura was not yet sure which way round it would be.

From one of their walks the two came back less happily than was usual. Charlotte had bought them each a large ice cream, and now she had a violent stomach-ache. She came humbly into the consulting-room, where Laura was fastening up a box of sleeping tablets.

'I've got this awful pain. Like a rip-rap exploding in my stomach all the time.'

Laura put a dab of sealing-wax on the paper. 'Have you ever had a rip-rap exploding in your stomach?'

'This is just what it must feel like.'

One of the many conclusions that Laura had reached after some years in general practice was that people who tried to describe pain were not suffering very greatly. Real pain was just pain: the sufferer would point, and say 'A pain — here.' No verbal flourishes. A pain.

She said: 'Probably indigestion.'

Charlotte explained about the ice cream, and Laura smiled mirthlessly. She reached up and took down a glass jar.

Charlotte said: 'The label's rubbed off. How do you know it's the right stuff?'

'I know what's in every bottle on these shelves,' said Laura. 'I could find any one in the dark if I had to. Unless,' she added, 'you've been moving them about while my back's been turned.'

'Of course I haven't. Why ever should I?'

Laura handed the draught to Charlotte, who tipped it back, and then screwed up her face.

'Ugh. Beastly.'

Like so many other patients, she did not bother to thank Laura. Really, she was so ordinary, ought one to feel any emotion about her at all? As a patient, she would not have aroused the faintest personal response from Laura.

But as the days went by, Laura realised

that she would never be truly calm until this situation was resolved. Small things irritated her; things that at one time she would have been able to shut out of her consciousness now nagged and pricked at her. In particular the sound of Charlotte's voice rasped. It struck some discordant resonance inside her head, so that she wanted to put her hands over her ears. But there was no ordinary way of shutting out that voice. It echoed on even when Charlotte was not there. Her laughter at a distance . . . the faint whisper of her chatter to Mrs. Swanton at the back of the house . . . the snatches of popular tunes she moaned to herself all day long . . . all these things seemed to get louder and louder, like a clamant radio that nightmarishly increased in volume and could not be turned off.

One morning towards the end of Mr. Drysdale's second week in hospital, Laura found herself staring at the scales on the bench. That weight — surely she could not have used that weight for the last lot of medicines she had made up?

She leaned over it, incredulous, and

found that she had sent Gilbert off with a package for one of her patients that contained a dose of phenobarbitone just ten times as strong as it ought to be.

It wouldn't kill the patient, but it would make him extremely sleepy. It was unwise to take chances. She got out the car and pursued Gilbert, who had set off on his bicycle ten minutes previously.

She caught him without difficulty. He looked surprised as she waved him in to the side.

'I've sent a wrong medicine,' she said. 'I must take it back and make sure the right one goes off tonight.'

He grinned, as though pleased to find that even she, whom he respected so much, could make mistakes. She nearly smiled back, suddenly seeing how easy it would be to like him — and then she was gripped by a searing pain, stirred by deep venomous anger at the mere idea.

'Put your bike in the back.'

With the hood down, it was easy to lay the bicycle over the back seat. Gilbert got in the front with her. She slewed the car savagely round, and drove back.

From the corner of her eye she was aware of him glancing tentatively at her. For the moment she could not say anything further to him. She was shocked by her own negligence. No one would know about it, and in any case there would have been no disastrous results. In spite of all the public panic and radio warnings about doctors who had left dangerous drugs in their cars, phenobarb was not as deadly as it was made out to be. But this indication of her lack of concentration was alarming. Something would have to be done. She must get herself out of this state. It was humiliating. She could afford to be vague no longer. She must act. Poison was accumulating in her system, working within her, distracting her. She must start releasing it.

It would have to be done. It wasn't her fault that she had to do this. *She* hadn't invited Charlotte to stay, had she? *She* hadn't wanted her here. *She* hadn't arranged for Mr. Drysdale to have such trouble with his veins and then to develop a varicose ulcer.

'You went to see your grandfather yesterday, didn't you?' she said in a level tone.

'That's right,' he said.

'How was everything?'

'He's doing very well, miss,' said Gilbert politely. 'Fussing about coming home.'

His face gave nothing away.

She said: 'Are you looking forward to having him home again?'

'Yes.'

'You wouldn't . . . ' The car drew up in front of the house. 'You wouldn't like to come and live here some day?'

'Here?' The echo was automatic, to gain time, but his eyes were revealing. He looked up at the prim square façade. There was uncertainty; there was bewilderment; but there was something else as well.

Laura said: 'Yes. How would you like to live here with . . . with your father?'

It was too abrupt. She had alarmed him.

'My father's dead,' he said.

'Are you quite sure?'

148

'Of course. Grandad told me.' But she sensed a wariness in his manner. With unexpected bitterness he blurted out: 'Of course there's one or two at school — they'd say anything — dirty lot.'

'What do they say?'

He was trembling. For a moment he shed the politeness he had always maintained. A manner he had acquired at school, and which he probably wore consistently among his friends there, rose suddenly like a cloak that he had pulled up around his shoulders. He snarled in the local accent:

'What's it got to do with you?'

'I'm your father's sister,' said Laura. She held open the door of the car. 'I think we'd better go in and talk about him.'

He remained motionless. She thought that when he moved he might run away. Then he shook his head pitifully and said:

'I don't know what you're talking about.'

He slid mechanically out of the seat, and in the same dazed way held the gate open for her. She went through. He followed her up the path.

'I'll tell you all about it,' said Laura pleasantly. 'It's all quite simple, really.'

They went into the consulting-room. She shut the door. They sat down, and she told him. It was as though she were discussing some pains he felt, explaining what they were and what they meant. But she did not yet suggest any appropriate treatment. Such recommendations would come later. Here and now she merely told him, calmly and clearly, about the past.

PART TWO

The potent poison quite o'ercrows my spirit.

1

He lay on his stomach, the sun hot on the back of his neck. Below him, pale pink trefoils flowered in early splendour across the surface of the still water. He stared at them. There was no movement.

It was early afternoon, and already the day had been too long. He had escaped from the house and the sound of voices, yet still Doctor Swanton's words seemed to pursue him. They would not leave him. In some ways it was worse out here; the rustling in the grass did not drown her voice as other voices might have done. He was exposed, defenceless.

A lark vibrated in the air a hundred yards away, then dropped. A couple of sheep bleated for a few moments, then lost interest and went on plucking away at the clover.

'I'm afraid,' Doctor Swanton was saying gently, 'we must face the fact that your father always had a weakness for that sort of woman.'

That sort of woman . . . His mother. And Charlotte.

He could not remember the order in which things had been said. They were all in his mind together now, not jumbled up but all there at once, clear and separate, so that he could distinguish each and every remark.

'I'm not saying that your grandfather was wrong to keep the truth from you. I'm sure he did what he thought was best. But you're old enough to know exactly what did happen — I think it may help you — and perhaps it will come better from me than from him.'

Not dead. His mother alive, his father alive. His mother had run off with an American. That was how little she had thought of him. 'That sort of woman.' And the dirty whispers, the vague suggestions that had once or twice been made to him in the school playground, were true.

He buried his face in the grass.

'I hope things are going to be different in the future. Your father is not a bad man. You'll like him. It's just that he's weak.'

Weak. Not meaning that he wasn't strong enough to work. Nothing like the meaning of 'weak' when scribbled by Miss Holyoake across home-work. Not illness — not what his grandfather meant when he said he felt weak and not up to doing much. It was something else: something he was old enough to grasp at. It was as disturbing as all the coarse jokes that you either ignored or laughed at, but that all left the same disquiet.

He wriggled, pushing himself up from the grass, turning on his side and letting his gaze wander over the bright beauty of the fields.

Weak. The sort of weakness that made you feel queer when you saw a girl with her head back, laughing in the middle of a group of boys . . . Or Charlotte raising her hand to push back her hair; Charlotte hurrying along the landing into her room.

'I can't say what will happen when your father comes home. But I hope we can keep him here. He needs a proper home. You might like to stay here, too — you'd be a help to him — but of course we can't settle things like that yet. Mrs. Swanton

— his wife — may have different ideas. It's too early to make plans.'

He could not make plans of any sort. Even the rest of this day was hard to work out. He dreaded going back to the house, dreaded facing them all. Yesterday and this morning had been awful. The immediate future might be worse. He felt that the weight on the top of his head was increasing. It was beginning to hurt, and would get worse.

The Easter holidays would soon be over. He must think about that. The holidays over, his grandfather back, everything would be all right. He would leave the Swantons and not see them again, not see them ever again if he could manage it.

He wondered if things could ever be really all right again.

He wondered what his father looked like.

'If it weren't for Charlotte, of course, there wouldn't be any question. You and your father could live here. We could all be together.'

He had not asked what would happen,

then, to his grandfather. He had asked very few questions. He had listened; or, rather, had left himself open to what she said, grasping the pieces and fitting them together only later, only now. At first it had all been unreal and had meant nothing. It was only during the night that he came to accept it. Now he wondered what she had meant and what she expected his grandfather to do. But that was not a serious problem. If the other details were sorted out, if Charlotte were (somehow, he did not ask how) not there, then nothing else would present any difficulty.

In any case, his grandfather was old. He would not last much longer.

Gil quivered as though a shock had run up from the earth through his fingers and arms. The rim of the dyke ahead of him blurred suddenly. He fell back, pressed himself to the ground again, and cried. There was no one to see or hear. He cried, and the tears trickled slowly over the hand he had put to his eyes and dropped into the grass.

It was the first time he had allowed

himself to think of his grandfather being old enough to be near death. Now he would never be entirely free from the thought again.

It wasn't Doctor Swanton's fault; and yet it would not have become so real to him if she had not spoken in that way. Only a few days ago — only yesterday morning, even — he had been free, and the world around Brookchurch had been wide and brilliant. Now it had all closed in on him.

He wiped the tears away, ashamed of his weakness.

Weakness . . . The word had new echoes.

He looked down at the ground. Among the flattened grasses was a crumpled yellow iris. Not so long ago Charlotte had asked him the name of that flower. They had laughed a lot and talked themselves hoarse that day. It wouldn't happen again like that.

Gil stopped trembling. He stood up and brushed the shreds of grass from his shirt and trousers. His mouth was set.

The village looked close at hand, but

was actually two miles away. A van flickered between the houses. He could see the Swanton house, looking as neat and square as it had always looked. But it was all wrong. As long as Charlotte was there — he couldn't explain this, but knew that it was what Doctor Swanton had meant, and somehow he agreed with her — as long as Charlotte went on living in that house, it would not be right. At the beginning he had felt she didn't belong. Now he was sure of it.

He wondered if he could ask Doctor Swanton to show him a picture of his father. There must be some in the house somewhere.

He felt that he could not ask yet.

As he walked back towards Brook-church, he hardened. There was nothing he wanted to say to anyone. Without consciously willing it, he began to develop a protective covering. He was walking stiffly, instinctively keeping his face set and unrevealing. Nobody could take him by surprise. He was not going to be taken unawares again — not by anything.

Charlotte was coming along the street

from the direction of the shops. She saw him, and waved.

He stopped.

Even at a distance she was too real. She wasn't something you could pretend wasn't there. He saw her arm fall, guessed her surprise that he had not waved back. She kept moving towards the house and kept watching him.

She was his mother. She and his mother were one and the same. The picture of his mother that stood on the cluttered mantelpiece in his grandfather's house became Charlotte. 'Both the same,' Doctor Swanton had said quietly, making him feel that this was an injection which was going to hurt, but he must be brave and in the end he would get better. ' . . . always had a weakness for that sort of woman.' Gil's mother, that sort of woman, had left him. Charlotte, for all her easy affection, for all the warmth of her laughter and the confiding touch of her hand on his arm, would leave him when she was ready. She wouldn't want to go on living down here. She would take his father away. She was that sort of woman.

Charlotte had reached the house and was waiting at the gate for him. He stayed where he was. She could not be wiped out. There she stood, and there she would be standing if he moved towards the house and went in. He could not blot her out by refusing to think of her; he could not even refuse to think of her.

He turned and blindly studied the bus time-table on the wall nearby. When at last he forced himself to look back at the house, Charlotte had disappeared.

He went slowly along the street.

Somewhere in the house there must be a picture of his father that he could find without having to ask Doctor Swanton for it.

2

Laura said: 'I really can't imagine why you've come, Mother.'

'I'm sure you're a very good doctor, my dear' — which was the nearest Mrs. Swanton would ever come to admitting that she was sometimes very far from sure of that fact — 'but you may overlook those little things . . . '

'What little things?'

'Oh,' said Mrs. Swanton, '*things*. Things that only a woman would notice.'

'And what am I supposed to be, pray?'

Mrs. Swanton did not reply. It was no use arguing with Laura. Anyway, that last remark was best left alone. In a way she had scored off Laura: by leaving the question to answer itself, she had got in a good one at Laura.

Poor girl, she thought with a sudden rush of affection. Poor girl; if only she *had* been a proper girl instead of aping her father — bless him — for all these years.

The car hummed down the last unexpectedly straight stretch of road into Tapton Harbour. They passed the small church, which seemed to have sunk even deeper into the shingle than when Mrs. Swanton had last seen it. But then, that had been nearly twenty years ago. It didn't bear thinking of. Twenty years since she had last been down to Tapton! It made her feel old, and rather feeble: she had become one of those marsh women they always used to laugh at, sitting tight in their houses or, at most, going down the street to the shops, shrivelling slowly up over the years, never venturing out into the wider spaces, never even visiting old friends a few miles away.

She remembered how, in the early days, Reginald had often brought her down here in the car. Sometimes she had walked across the fields alone, or with Peter and Laura when they were small. She could do the same today: she was not yet old; but somehow she had never considered it. She had allowed herself to sink into a sort of retirement — one might almost have called it a retreat — on

Reginald's death, and had been thankful for Laura's need of her. She had worked for Laura, and it had kept her going. The house was the same, the routine the same as it had always been; and Laura needed to be waited on and pandered to as much as Reginald had done, though the job was less rewarding and Laura lacked her father's grave, courteous manner and that slow smile which had always made everything worth while.

'Wake up,' said Laura. 'If you're determined to come in, that is.'

They had stopped outside the end house in the row that Mrs. Swanton knew as Pits Lane. In her memory there had never been an actual road, and in some way it reassured her to find that even now there was still only a broad, lumpy shingle path before the houses. At the end of the row the shingle dribbled away into a track which went on through the spiky marram grass towards the green-flecked pools below the sea wall.

Things here had not changed too much.

The past was even more vivid and

immediate when Gilbert held the door open and the two women went into Mr. Drysdale's cottage. Though perhaps vivid was not the right word: the interior was faded, the wallpaper was a dark jungle of sombre flowers, the cloth on the table was of heavy green chenille, and the window curtains seemed to shut out the light even when they were drawn back.

Mrs. Swanton recognised so many things here. There was Lucy's clock on the mantelpiece, still keeping good time; and that picture of cows knee-deep in a stream — cows, stream and background alike all speckled with brown — had hung in Lucy's home when she was a girl.

'Well, fancy *you* comin' all this way,' said Mr. Drysdale. 'Gilbert, make us a pot of tea like a good lad.'

'Show me where everything is, and I'll do it,' said Mrs. Swanton, her smile claiming Gil as an old friend who did not have to stand on ceremony with her.

But his answering smile was gravely formal, and he went out at once into the little kitchen, closing the door behind him.

'Well, how's the leg?' asked Laura. In her bag was a letter from the consultant, but she automatically invited the invalid to say his piece.

Mr. Drysdale shifted in his chair, his leg stiffly out in front of him. 'All right, I reck'n.' The reply was grudging, as though he was not prepared to commit himself too definitely in case he should wish to retract later. 'Stiff, though,' he added threateningly.

'Let me have a look.'

'More proddin' and quizzin',' said Mr. Drysdale. He glanced at Mrs. Swanton. Her presence made him less respectful towards Laura than he was ordinarily: even less was she Doctor Swanton today, even more was she just Bella Swanton's daughter.

'Hm,' said Laura. 'Full of phlebitis. Only to be expected.'

'You told me as everythin' 'ud be all right once I'd got that operation over with —'

'It won't do you any harm to take things easy.'

'Never did have time to take things

easy.' His stare in Mrs. Swanton's direction became a scowl.

She said placatingly: 'Gilbert will be able to give you a lot of help. He's grown up to be a very nice boy. You must be proud of him.'

'If I am, I reck'n I'm the only one who's got any right to be.'

There was an uncomfortable pause. Mrs. Swanton broke it by saying: 'Mind you let us know if you need anything. I expect I could run down once a week just to . . . well, tidy up and so on.'

Mr. Drysdale looked appalled. The two women were harassing him beyond endurance. 'No call to do that,' he said gruffly.

'Gilbert can always drop in on his way home from school if you've got a message for us — '

'He'll be doing that anyway,' said Laura.

Mr. Drysdale stared from one to the other. He said: 'You're not countin' on keepin' Gil on, are you? Not now?'

'Of course not,' said Mrs. Swanton with a quick frown at Laura. 'He must come home to look after you.'

'But he can still call in on us on his way home,' said Laura flatly, 'and do the odd jobs.'

'Really, Laura, I'm sure it would be better if — '

'The money will come in useful,' said Laura to Mr. Drysdale.

He wriggled into his chair, pushing himself back as though to get a good support for himself before he spoke.

'The lad looks as though he . . . he's glad to be back home. Don't think he fancies carryin' on.'

Mrs. Swanton bridled. The implications of that remark seemed singularly ungracious to her. 'Obviously Gil enjoyed himself while he was with us, but we wouldn't dream of leaving you on your own — we wouldn't want him to waste his time on odd jobs when you're likely to need him so much.'

Laura said deliberately: 'When Gilbert looks for a job in the summer, he'll probably want a reference from us.'

'It'd do some good,' Mr. Drysdale agreed. 'I'd be much obliged — '

'It's going to be difficult to give him a reference if he packs up at the first excuse. If he's bored with the small jobs he does for us, isn't he going to be bored elsewhere?'

Mrs. Swanton could not believe her ears. She could not make out what had got into Laura. 'Laura, whatever are you talking about?'

'I think he ought to stay with us for a while, after we've looked after him as we have done. I think it's the least he can do.'

'If he don't want to carry on, he don't have to.' The decisiveness of Mr. Drysdale's tone showed how uncertain he was about the whole affair.

He seemed, during his weeks in hospital, to have shrunk. He did not look ill, but it was as though that brief imprisonment, away from his usual surroundings, had frightened him and given rise to a lot of doubts where there had never before been any doubts. He looked from Laura to her mother as though they were stronger than he and might do something against his wishes, outflanking him and giving him no chance to resist.

Mrs. Swanton clucked her tongue. 'Really, what *are* we getting so cross about?'

The door was pushed open by Gil's foot. He came in with a tray on which were three cups of tea and a sugar bowl. They were all at once silent, watching as he set the tray down. Then he turned to the sideboard and took out a biscuit tin.

'Bring a cup in for yourself, Gil,' said his grandfather.

Gil looked at him — but not at the others — and smiled. 'I think I'd better finish chopping up those boxes.'

He was quiet and very final. He turned and went out, and the door closed quietly behind him.

Mr. Drysdale said: 'What you been doin' to him while I been away?'

'*Doing* to him?' Mrs. Swanton was again indignant.

'He's . . . shut himself off. He's growed up.'

Laura stood with her back to the empty grate, sipping tea in large gulps in her usual way. One would have thought there had just been an emergency call and this might be her last cup of tea for some hours. Yet at the same time, thought her mother, she looked firmly established here — firmly dug in, with no intention of leaving until everything was settled to her satisfaction.

'I certainly think Gilbert should carry on with us for a while,' said Laura. 'He might not feel ready for another job yet. If, as you say, he has matured since he's been with us, that's all to the good. I'm glad to hear it.'

'I'm not so sure — '

'Oh, nonsense, Laura,' said Mrs. Swanton. 'Of course he can't stay with us. There's no future in it for a boy like him.'

Laura did not trouble to answer. She finished her tea and set the cup and saucer down with a rattle.

Mrs. Swanton covertly studied her. She knew that expression on Laura's face. Laura looked like that when a case puzzled her but did not entirely defeat her: when she knew deep down what was wrong, but could not get the details in focus. It had happened so often. She would come in, fretful, after a visit, and look ahead of her in just that glazed, intimidating way. Some time later — it might be five minutes or five hours — she would nod abruptly and say 'Of course . . . I knew it all along.' And invariably she would be right. At such times Mrs. Swanton was awed by her daughter. She knew that such results were produced by the analytical workings of the trained mind, by wheels turning even when Laura herself was unconscious of them; but even so there was something uncanny about it all.

Why should she look like that now? She was diagnosing a situation, feeling her way . . . and in due course — how long would it take? — she would nod and say 'Yes, that's it, there we are.'

Now, abruptly, she said: 'I shall be very upset if you stop Gilbert coming in to help each evening, Mr. Drysdale.'

'Well, it's not a matter of me stoppin' him. I mean . . . well . . . '

Mrs. Swanton wagged her head, bewildered. She was convinced that Laura did not yet understand her own reasons for insisting that Gilbert should continue to come. There was something disturbing about that dogged insistence, as though she hoped by persevering to reach the right diagnosis.

Diagnosis, treatment of *what*? Mrs. Swanton had never understood Laura and never would; but she felt that, for some reason, she was right to be uneasy.

Gilbert came back into the room. It was true that he was different. A sort of veil had fallen over his face. He was more deliberate in his speech, giving the impression that he checked each word before it was uttered. His eyes were unyouthfully cold and calculating as he looked from his grandfather to Laura and then to Mrs. Swanton.

Mr. Drysdale said: 'Just in time. Been talkin' about you.'

'Oh.'

'Now, then' — Mr. Drysdale was bluff and loud, insistent on a clear reply and no nonsense — 'how d'you feel about goin' on workin' for the doctor? Want to keep on a bit, eh?'

'I don't think so,' said Gilbert steadily.

Laura leaned forward. Gil turned

towards her. For a moment his eyes challenged hers, then he flushed and looked down.

She said: 'I'm sorry to hear that, Gil. I thought you liked being with us.'

'I liked it all right.' His shrug was a boy's shrug of embarrassment, and his mouth was sullen in a boyish way. Mrs. Swanton felt immediately sorry for him.

Not so Mr. Drysdale. Mr. Drysdale blew down his nose, and his voice became hard and inexplicably womanish. A proper old granny, thought Mrs. Swanton involuntarily.

'This is a fine thing, I must say. You youngsters today, you get fed up with a job in no time. We couldn't afford to be so choosey when I was a lad, *I* can tell you. How do you think you'll hold down a man's job if you can't abide this little one?'

'It's not that.'

'What is it, then? What sort of reference do you think Doctor Swanton is going to write you if you leave just like that?'

Gilbert glanced at the window. The shingle cast back the sunlight, hard and exuberant. His lips parted, and he looked as though he wanted to appeal to someone to intervene.

Laura said again: 'I thought you liked being with us.'

'I did.' He looked straight at her. 'But you know, you know what it is. I don't want to come back.'

Laura was silent. Mr. Drysdale groaned, and shifted in his chair. He looked puzzled — puzzled with all of them and with himself, wondering whose side he was on and what had happened to start this.

Suddenly Gilbert put one hand on his shoulder. His voice was thick and uncertain.

'I want to stay here,' he said.

Tears smarted inexplicably in Mrs. Swanton's eyes. It was as though the boy were afraid of something — of losing his grandfather, of not being here if anything happened to him . . . of something secret and personal that had nothing to do with chopping wood and emptying buckets of ash and getting a job.

Mr. Drysdale said: 'Damn it, if you don't want to go there every night, you don't have to.'

Mrs. Swanton looked at Laura. Laura's expression had not changed. She continued to look thoughtful and strangely remote as she picked up her bag and got ready to leave.

3

Charlotte was waiting for the bus. This was the second time this week that she had been into Jury. The need to escape from the house grew more pressing every day.

She looked down the Tapton Harbour road, along which the bus would come; and, looking in that direction, thought inevitably of Gil.

She could not understand what had happened. That he should have returned home to look after his grandfather was only to be expected. But that he should have made it so clear that he did not want to see her again was humiliating. For a boy to look at her as he had looked at her, to turn away with that shiver as though disgusted with her or with himself . . . it was hateful.

Even before he had got ready to leave it was plain that their agreeable, undemanding comradeship had been destroyed. Not only did he not seek her out, or turn to grin at her as she passed: he deliberately avoided her. She was surprised how much this rankled. There were evenings when she was at a loose end and would have welcomed his company. But either he was not to be found or he had some job to do for Laura — 'Rather specially want to get it done right now,' he would say, not looking at her, looking anywhere but straight at her.

It was almost a relief when the time came for him to go home.

Charlotte had intercepted him on his last evening in the Swanton house. She was angry that she should be forced to lie in wait for him, as though he were a man who had wearied of her, and she a woman who must make one last pitiful attempt to appeal to him. She stood in the waiting-room, not making a sound, for nearly ten minutes, and emerged as he came down the stairs.

She said: 'So you're off, Gil.'

He was holding a case in his right hand. It was heavy, but he did not put it down when she spoke to him. He stood at the foot of the stairs and looked towards the side door.

'Yes,' he said.

'I . . . I hope we don't lose touch.'

He said nothing.

'I expect your grandfather will need you a lot at first,' said Charlotte desperately. 'But after that you'll be coming in and out again, I suppose?'

'I don't know,' he said.

'We must go out for some more walks when you've got some time.' Really, she ought to stop; but she could not. 'Perhaps I can drop in and see you and your grandfather one week-end when you're at home.'

To this he absolutely refused to reply. The case swung slowly in his hand and jarred against his thigh.

Charlotte said: 'Gil, what's the matter?'

'The matter, miss?' His innocence was blank, hard and unyielding.

And so he went.

Later, she learned that he would not be returning to the house at all: he would not even be calling in to do the odd jobs for which he had originally been engaged. This had all been decided a few days after he had gone, at some meeting, some-where, at some time when she was not present. Laura told her the news with apparent indifference, but seemed to derive some satisfaction from studying her reaction.

The bus appeared far down the road. It would take her to the town, and there she could look at the shops and have a cup of coffee and look at more shops, and fritter away an afternoon. Then there would be surgery, and then the radio — if Laura didn't come into the sitting-room; Laura could not bear to have the radio on.

The bus turned at the foot of the church tower, and slowed.

She would much sooner have gone out across the marsh. But not alone. She would have been plagued by the recollection of Gil's face and his earnest, sometimes derisive, explanatory voice; she would have remembered, against her will, the change in that voice — the contempt which had seeped into it. The town was better.

The bus carried her away from Brookchurch.

It stopped at a crossroads, and two women from a nearby farm climbed in. They were at once involved in shrill conversation with another woman who might, if one could judge from the enthusiasm with which she was greeted, have come from the other side of the world.

They were strangers to Charlotte. She knew nobody who was not in the closest contact with the Swantons, and even then the acquaintanceship was sketchy in the extreme. The woman at Duckett's farm, the grocer, and one of the girls beyond the post office counter were the only ones she spoke to at all regularly. She had not tried to make friends. Let them point her out as 'Mrs. Swanton — you know, that Peter Swanton, the one who's in gaol.' They should come no closer.

She stared unseeingly out of the window.

Leave. You're not wanted here.

That had been made plain in so many ways, hadn't it?

The bus climbed from the marsh into Jury, through the ancient gateway, and at last into the market square.

The first thing Charlotte did this

afternoon was go and look at the times of trains for London.

She had never been good at interpreting railway time-tables. Many a journey she had intended to make had been abandoned simply because those patterns of figures had refused to fall into coherent shape. A feeling of frustration came over her whenever she tried with a despairing finger to trace the progress of a train that came from one place into a junction to meet a connection which would, in its turn, head roughly in the direction she wanted.

Today the hieroglyphics were as baffling as ever. A train that came from farther along the coast ought to stop at Jury and then, rationally speaking, go on to . . . where on earth did it go from here? She closed her eyes for an instant. Perhaps when she opened them again her forefinger would be resting on an intelligible column; perhaps, like someone picking out texts or horses with a pin, she would be given guidance and prodded into action.

But departures from Jury and arrivals

at Charing Cross just would not add up. It seemed that all trains leaving this town ran off the rails somewhere in the Weald of Kent and were lost from human sight.

She tried to summon up the determination to go and make enquiries at the booking-office.

From down the line came a whistle. The bridge over the river hummed, the level-crossing rattled, and then steam blew over the roof of the station. At the same moment an army lorry turned into the station approach and stopped with a jolt, its tailboard chains clattering.

Charlotte moved away from the time-table. She was always disturbed and excited by people boarding or leaving a train. As they came through the door now, giving up tickets, she glanced swiftly at their faces as though waiting for someone she knew; in reality she was hoping to seize something that would help her — some message, some revelation from the world that lay far away down the railway line.

A group of young soldiers squashed through the door. Their raw necks emerged querulously from their battle-dress. They humped their kitbags out of the way of a porter, and the driver of the three-ton lorry came towards them.

'You lot for the egg farm?'

Behind them came an older man in uniform, carefully separate from them. He looked idly round, jerked his head in Charlotte's direction, and then said:

'Long time no see. You wouldn't be waiting for me?'

She was startled by his jaunty, impudent smile. Then she remembered the pub at Tapton Harbour, and forced an answering smile.

'Er, no,' she said. 'No, I'm afraid not.'

'Well, all right. Just my luck. I didn't really think you would be.'

He was deeply sunburnt, and his teeth flashed white. He seemed full of energy: he stood with his head thrust slightly forward, as though ready to provoke a fight or an argument. It would take a lot to shake that expression of aggressive self-satisfaction.

Charlotte heard herself saying: 'I owe you a drink, don't I?'

'Do you? Well, anyway, we've just got time for one.'

There was no waste of time. He did not look flattered that she had remembered him or that she had not rebuffed him. His policy was to take everything for granted the moment it had happened, and to press on. He was already steering her across the station approach, with that swagger of his that had more in common with a sailor's rolling gait than the usual army saunter.

'I was really thinking of having a cup of coffee,' said Charlotte.

'Were you, now? This'll do you more good. May as well celebrate the end of my leave in good style.'

'You've just come back from leave?' she banally said.

'Back to the spud-bashing,' he said.

'Did you have a good time?'

He smacked his lips lightly. 'Good?' he said with a grimace. 'Good? You don't know the half of it.' The remark pleased him. 'You don't know the half of it,' he repeated, with a depth of meaning that was significant only to himself.

His eyes flickered appraisingly over Charlotte, and he looked even more delighted with himself as they entered the saloon bar. Charlotte wondered what had prompted her to make that remark about owing him a drink. She had not really intended to come into a pub with him; had not meant to be drawn into anything at all.

But his confident smile was soothing. Smug and irritating, yet soothing.

She put her handbag on a vacant chair, and took out her purse.

'Will you get them, please?'

'That's all right,' he said.

'Please.'

He did not argue further, but took the money from her and went to the bar. Charlotte stretched out her right foot and looked down at her white shoe, coated with a slight film of dust. She tweaked at her flowered, light green skirt, and then ran her right hand thoughtfully up her bare left arm. She might have been gently restoring the circulation: she felt herself coming slowly, warily to life.

When he had sat down opposite,

grinning at her, she said:

'I think you told me your name was Walter, last time we met.'

'If I did, I was dead right. Didn't have time to tell you much else, the way you hustled off.' The window above them darkened as the three-tonner came in close to the kerb on the corner. 'New batch,' he said. 'Poor blighters.'

'Oughtn't you to have been on that lorry?'

'Not me. Not due back till twenty-four-hundred. It's just that the train services to this dump are so lousy: you've got to get back early. Not that I'm sorry to be back, right now.'

The compliment was offered in the certainty that it would be appreciated.

Charlotte thoroughly appreciated it. She was in no mood to be critical. She felt a fleeting twinge of fear at the unlikely prospect of Laura appearing suddenly in the doorway, as had happened once before. Then it faded. She had no reason to be afraid of Laura. She was not going to accept Laura's standards all the time. In a way, she would almost have been pleased to be seen here.

Then the barman was calling, 'Time, gentlemen, please. Time, ladies and gents.'

She looked at Walter. He winked. 'Nice afternoon,' he said. 'Just right for a boat on the river.'

'I didn't know they had any boats — '

'Ah.' He put his glass down and tapped the side of his nose. She noticed how thick and yellow his nails were. 'Not for the general public. You've got to be in the know.'

'And you're in the know?' She gave him his cue.

'I can fix it,' he said. 'Leave it to me.'

Fifteen minutes later they were floating out into the middle of the sand-cloudy river. Insects bounced across the surface, and the sun sparkled in the drops of water that fell from the oars.

Walter's delight was infectious. He had made some quick, efficient arrangement for leaving his case at a shop in the town, had joked with the man who owned the skiff, and was now pulling with strong rhythmical strokes on the oars. You could, as he had invited, leave it to him.

'It's pretty public,' he said as the town slowly receded. 'Not much privacy along here.'

His head was lowered as he bent forward on the oars, so that he was looking up at her from under his eyebrows as though the sun were in his eyes.

'Yes,' she said non-committally.

She did not want to think things out or talk about the possible consequences of this present situation. The drowsy plash of the water was enough. Enough for now.

'Summer's coming,' said Walter brightly.

The weather was not really warm, but there was no longer that chill which had lain on things for so many months. The river curled lazily in, away from the plain, and the long shallow valley twisted away into the hazy afternoon, its flanks sprouting an occasional cluster of farm buildings and white jutting oast-houses. Charlotte trailed her hand in the water, and shivered with pleasure.

Walter pulled on one oar and steered them in to the bank. Pollarded trees rose like stunted sentinels above. There was no shade.

'Well,' said Walter expansively. 'Well.'

For the first time he showed a flicker of uncertainty. 'Here we are,' he said.

Here they were. The river, the bank, the flat fields, the remote sky, the unsheltering hills: what did they add up to; to what were they supposed to provide a background?

'We could get out,' said Walter.

'If you like,' said Charlotte.

He clambered on to the bank, and secured the boat to the bole of a tree. Then he helped her out, his right hand firm in hers. She stumbled. His left hand caught her at the waist and steadied her. She saw, closely, the odd configuration of wrinkles under his eyes, and the thickness of his lips, and she neatly released herself.

They sat down.

She had not expected to feel so utterly indifferent. The entire landscape had lost its colour: it stretched away in endless monochrome, and she closed her eyes against it. She sat upright on the grass with her eyes tightly shut. When, after a few seconds, she opened them, she saw that Walter had sprawled out beside her.

He was fumbling in his pocket for a cigarette case and lighter.

The background was meaningless; and the foreground, too, had lost its significance — if it had ever had any. She felt frightened. She had allowed herself to drift into this situation, and now was unable to jerk herself out of this mood of indifference.

Walter grinned at her.

Walter was real. He looked at her as though she, too, were real. She needed someone like Walter. He was gloriously, healthily uncomplicated. She wanted him to start talking again so that she could listen to the London echoes in his voice.

She said: 'What do you do down at the ranges?'

'Ah, that's hush hush. Official secrets. Anyhow, it's not what I do down there that matters. What I do with my spare time is more interesting.'

He spoke slightly more quickly, with a flattering urgency in his voice. They looked at one another, solemn for a moment. Then he pushed himself up, stubbed out his cigarette in the grass, and kissed her.

She closed her eyes. His breath had the sourness of tobacco and a journey; he seemed to breathe life in through her parted lips.

She was glad that her blouse was so flimsy, so that his hand was close to her.

When he drew away, she smiled.

'Well, now,' he said huskily. 'Well.'

He got up and looked desperately across the flat landscape. She did not move. She waited, her palms pressed down against the grass, exulting in this tingling sensation of being fully alive and responsive.

Walter was devoured by impatience. She was not troubled. Somehow she knew that this welcome hunger could not fail to be appeased.

He said: 'There's a hut over there, isn't there?'

'A looker's hut, probably,' she lazily said.

'A what?'

'A looker's hut. A looker — one of the shepherds round these parts. I don't know if they use them much.'

'Not at this time of year, anyway,' said

Walter. He took her hand roughly. 'Come on.'

They walked across the blazing field, stumbling and beginning to laugh pointlessly.

Charlotte said: 'I hardly know you.'

'No,' he said, not looking at her. 'No, you don't, do you?'

She sensed his apprehensiveness as they approached the tiny brick building. The door might be locked. The place might be filthy inside.

But the door creaked and lurched open. There was some rather smelly straw on the ground, and a couple of tarpaulins or rolled sheets of some sort in one corner.

Walter pushed the door shut. The atmosphere was warm, acrid, too long enclosed.

Charlotte sneezed.

Walter pulled her close to him. The button on his top pocket was hard against her breast. His fingers moved restlessly on her back.

When she could get her mouth free she said: 'I'm not going to get scratched by all that straw and stuff.'

'All right, all right.' He began to unfasten his battledress blouse.

She watched him for a moment. Her knees felt weak. Then she put up one hand and unfastened the top button of her own blouse.

Her shoulders were very white against his brown, rather leathery skin.

'Suppose someone looked in at the window?' she said, laughing.

He looked up at the dusty pane. 'I'll breathe on it if you like, so they can't see.'

She went on laughing. He joined her, and then abruptly put his mouth on hers to silence her. For a moment they were quite still; then he moved upon her.

She was, all the time, clearly conscious of the tilted roof and the cobwebs on the window. When his hard hands released their grip on her and she was free, she felt oddly unconcerned. Almost she wondered what circumstances had brought her into this queer little place.

She sat up and said, with a matter-of-factness that was somehow nothing to do with her real self:

'We really ought to be going.'

'There's no great panic,' said Walter.

She picked up his blouse and dropped it on him.

'Come on.'

He was puzzled, but her smile reassured him. He got up with a disgruntled moan, and tried to kiss her again, but it was light and meaningless.

They went back to the skiff. She felt, strangely, much closer to him on the journey back than she had done in the hut. When he said with a brightness that did not quite conceal his momentary uncertainty, 'Free some evening next week — Tuesday, say?' she nodded.

'We'll have more time on Tuesday,' he said.

She could foresee that by Tuesday he would have something organised. 'Organised' — it was a word he himself would use and approve of.

She felt a tremor of anticipation. She had spent too long a time in the company of women. There simply had to be a change; there had to be something to keep her alive until Peter was released;

there had to be *somebody*.

Peter would have understood.

And who was Peter to complain, after all she had learned about him recently?

Peter was far away.

Now that they were approaching the town, once more across the flashing surface of the water, she wished she could have been more responsive in the hut. But it had been so long — she had not been ready, not . . . not in practice, she wanted to giggle out loud.

Next time would be different.

Damn Laura, damn her cold eyes and her hard mouth, damn her for bringing Gil to the house and then sending him away.

Going back in the bus, Charlotte found that for no good reason she was despondent and wanted to cry.

4

Summer was dubious yet insistent. It hesitated and seemed about to succumb to discouragement, allowing a blustering wind and rain to gain the ascendancy. Then, a day later, there would be an appreciable advance: the grass would be dry under the suddenly aggressive sun, and the distances would shimmer like water.

The older folk of the district developed their usual seasonal complaints. Their rheumatism, about which they had made such bitter prophecies at the onset of winter, began to give them even more trouble. There were streaming colds — 'An' no wonder, what wi' rain one day and sun the next' — and a minor epidemic of influenza. Laura predicted the deaths of two old women who had, some months ago, declared that they would not survive the winter. Her predictions were fulfilled. Having survived the winter, the patients viewed the coming of summer with a feeling almost of resentment, and decided to die.

There was an outbreak of polio some ten miles away. It spread insidiously. Parents kept their children away from school — but not from the cinema — and Laura was called out to some few dozen urgent cases which proved to be no more than ordinary sore throats, stiff necks, or the result of sheer imagination. Also, she watched a child die.

Someone was run over fifty yards from their front door. Charlotte saw the stains, shrouded in sawdust, after the casualty had been removed. It made her sick. She thought how Peter would have felt, and contrasted him with his sister.

'I don't know how you do it,' she said to Laura.

There was awe in her tones. She was prepared, Laura realised, to admire — prepared to look up to her.

So many of them were like that. Even those not directly concerned were willing, even anxious, to idolise a doctor in the hour of need. One learned not to react to their worshipping eyes, their silly admiration. She had learned early. She had never gone through that sentimental stage of wanting to do good, to nurse the sick, to lay a cool hand on a fevered brow . . .

For Laura, sickness was a challenge. She fought to save people's lives merely in order to feel that she had cheated death: she battled to drive it from the room. Success gave her a thrill of power and achievement. When she lost, there would invariably be a moment of black frustration — then nothing. The dead were always so dead. Once life had fled, there was so clearly nothing left . . . nothing at all. The job was finished. She lost interest at once. They called her callous; yet they recognised, as she knew with pride, her untiring determination: they relied, those who became her patients, on that will of hers, preferring her unsparing, angry devotion to the pleasantly soothing ministrations of Dr. Whiting.

Laura drew few generalisations from her work. A case was a case, she dealt with its various features, and she formulated no philosophy. Only now and then did she allow herself, impatiently, to resent the outcome of a particular struggle.

'All the better people die,' she once said to her mother, in a rare moment of confidence. 'The ones who are useful, and who have responsibilities — they die. When I see those that are left, and think of what some of them deserve — '

'You shouldn't talk like that, dear. And besides' — Mrs. Swanton threw it in as a consolation — 'the bad ones go too, all in due time. We all come to it.'

The bad ones go, too. Laura sat at her desk one bright afternoon and thought about that. Yes, they would all go in time; but some of them not soon enough.

Charlotte, for example. How much better the world would be without Charlotte! She might so easily succumb to one of the many seasonal ailments — or to something far more serious. Other people did. But Charlotte went on unscathed. It was quite wrong.

Laura rubbed her eyes. She was more tired than she cared to admit. She rarely enjoyed the summer months: warm languorous days had never appealed to her. In the cold weather she could be brisk and wide awake. Now she was too easily exhausted.

She ought to be getting out that bottle and nasal dropper for Mrs. Thompson. And there were at least two other visits she simply must fit in this afternoon.

There was a tap at the door. Her mother looked in with a placatory smile. In the passage, standing in shadow, was Charlotte.

'Anything you want in Jury, dear?' asked Mrs. Swanton.

'Not that I can think of,' said Laura, surprised. 'Why?'

'Charlotte's going in on the next bus. We thought . . . she thought she might get anything you wanted. Save you a journey.'

It was a blatant bid for affection. Who had thought of it — her mother, or Charlotte? Probably mother. This was one of her sporadic attempts to persuade the two of them (and herself; perhaps herself above all) that really they were getting on splendidly together.

Mrs. Swanton looked anxious when she

did not get an immediate reply. She ventured:

'Charlotte was saying how tired you've been looking.'

Charlotte, obviously making an effort, edged forward.

'I thought if I could do anything while I was out shopping . . . '

Laura pushed herself up from her chair. 'If you mean you want a lift into Jury, why not say so?'

'Really, Laura,' protested her mother: 'the way you twist things!'

Laura reached up for the bottle and dropper for Mrs. Thompson, and walked towards Charlotte.

'Coming, then?'

Charlotte flushed, and her limp little mouth tightened. She swung abruptly round and walked out. They heard her cross the waiting-room, and the front door slammed behind her.

'Really, Laura,' said Mrs. Swanton again.

Laura went out at a more leisurely pace. She got into the car, and turned towards Jury.

On the corner by the church, Charlotte was standing at the bus-stop.

Laura could not repress a smile. Flouncing out of the house in a flurry of indignation, Charlotte had forgotten that the next bus was not due for another twenty minutes. She had condemned herself to a long wait.

Laura brought the car in to the kerb. Charlotte turned away.

'Come on,' said Laura. 'Get in.'

'I'm not in any hurry,' said Charlotte.

'Don't be silly. Get in.'

There was no one about; no one to witness what would happen or not happen. Proud defiance meant nothing on an empty stage.

'I've got to go through Jury anyway,' said Laura. 'You can get the bus back. It'll give you a lot more time if you come in with me.' Her amused contempt for Charlotte was so great that she found she could feel almost charitable towards her.

Charlotte got in. The car swung round the corner and raced inland.

The breeze was hot. Laura narrowed her eyes against the brightness of the glistening road. Charlotte sat bolt upright and stared straight ahead.

A blaze of rambler roses fell in a torrent over a wall where the car slowed for a bend. Beyond a low gate shone a Georgian house, expansive in its ideal setting, its ideal summer afternoon.

'That's a lovely house,' said Laura idly. She carried the picture of it in her mind as they drove on: a picture of this afternoon, given an added dimension by memory. 'Peter,' she said, 'used to say he'd live there one day.'

'Daydreams,' said Charlotte. 'I remember I — '

'He used to make up stories about the place. He liked the shutters and the look of the front door. We never passed it without something new occurring to him.'

'He'll have forgotten all that by now.'

'I don't think so. You never forget things like that. Childhood impressions are much more important than anything that comes later. They cause a lot of trouble, one way and another.'

'Peter's got over being troubled by that sort of thing,' said Charlotte tightly.

Laura's brief mood of tolerance faded. The pert hostility of Charlotte's voice had begun once more to rasp on her nerves. She said:

'No one can get away from the past. Certainly Peter can't. I know him. His childhood, his family, his daydreams . . . they can't be cancelled out. They'll always be there. Whether you cling to your memories or repudiate them, they've had their effect on you. When Peter comes back here — '

'Peter isn't coming back here,' said Charlotte.

Jury scrambled up the hill ahead of them. Laura drove faster and faster, then slowed at the speed limit sign.

She said: 'Where do you suppose he can go, then?'

'Not here,' said Charlotte urgently. 'Anywhere but here. He's not going to come back. I won't let him.'

'He may have ideas of his own about that. We'll see.'

'No,' said Charlotte. 'No. This place has done him enough harm. It's not going to do him any more. I'm never going to let him come back here, not now I know what it's like. Never.'

The swirl of traffic at the foot of the slope caught them up. A double-decker bus leaned out from the corner, and Laura drove with angry precision between its green wall and the rattling side of an oncoming builder's lorry. She went up into the main shopping street, and stopped for a few seconds only to let Charlotte get out. Neither of them spoke again. Laura drove on, over the hill and out of the town, swinging back at last on to the marsh below.

She visited Mrs. Thompson and two other patients, spent about five minutes in each house, and afterwards did not remember what she had said. She did not remember driving down the road to Brookchurch, but in a space of time which she could not have measured she found herself back at her desk.

'Is that you, dear?' Mrs. Swanton called from the back of the house. 'There's been a call for you. I've left the message on your pad.'

Laura read the message and pushed it

to one side. She pulled the filing tray towards her and went through the accumulation of letters and advertising pamphlets. Discarded material she stacked on one side, and then began to tear it up, four or five letters and glossy circulars at a time, folding them and tearing them across with a savage twist of her wrists.

If only something would happen. If only fate would contrive an accident . . . *something*. But she did not believe in fate, beneficent or malevolent.

Peter's marriage to Charlotte was a thing which ought not to last. But Laura had in these recent years seen so much sickness, so much pain and stupidity, so much that was senseless, purposeless, that she knew the marriage would probably last for year after intolerable year. They were both healthy, and one felt they would avoid the more common accidents. Peter would be bound irremediably to Charlotte unless something happened — or, rather, unless something were *made* to happen.

On the other side of the wall she heard a dull thump. Then there was a scrabbling noise that seemed to come up from under the floor, a noise like the rustling of innumerable beetles in the foundations.

It was a familiar sound, but for a moment it puzzled Laura. She was not usually here when this part of the day's routine was carried out. As a rule Gil had gone down to the cellar to fill the scuttle for the fire when she was out on her visits. Now that he no longer came, Laura's mother did the job. It was Mrs. Swanton who at this moment was scraping and shovelling away in the cellar.

I suppose, thought Laura — by no means for the first time — we ought to get an electric water heater and save all that clambering up and down. But — the answer came as it had come every time before — the stove does heat the house so beautifully, and once they started ripping it out there was no telling . . .

She shook herself, and then got up. These disjointed thoughts were as irritating as the ramblings of some patient coming out from under an anæsthetic.

She heard her mother's feet dragging up the ladder, and the bump of the scuttle on the floor of the passage. Then the footsteps went heavily away.

As usual, Mrs. Swanton had forgotten to close the flap of the cellar behind her. She seemed to have a rooted objection to doing so until she had carried the scuttle out to the kitchen. Gil had always been most meticulous about that, ever since Laura had given him the severe little lecture which she had also, so many times, without result, given to her mother.

'The passage is very dark, Mother. You know yourself what it's like for anyone coming in from outside. The whole thing is a case of real incompetence: it ought never to have been made in that way.'

'It was your father, dear, who had it put in,' her mother would gently remind her. 'It was to save us going out of doors and down the steps at the back.'

Gil had not argued or grumbled about bad design. He had nodded, and made a point of closing the flap as soon as he emerged.

'Of course,' Laura had said to her mother more than once, 'if you *want* to get rid of me — if you *want* me to break my neck . . . '

She was about to open the door now and go out and down the passage, to slam the flap so that her mother would hear it and feel guilty, when a sound made her stop.

There were quick footsteps at the front of the house. She looked out of the window, and realised that several hours had somehow escaped her. The afternoon was at its end, and Charlotte was coming back towards the house.

It was still sunny outside. Laura knew what it would be like to enter the house from that bright world — first the coolness of the waiting-room, with sunlight striking in at angles, and then the darkness of the passage to the kitchen. The eyes were not ready for that plunge into shadow: one screwed them up and walked into darkness towards the renewed brightness of the kitchen at the end.

The flap over the steps down into the cellar was up. Propped sideways against the wall, it did not cut off the rectangle of light from the kitchen door. To leave that flap open like that was to invite an accident.

Laura stood quite still with her hand on the doorknob. She heard Charlotte come in and cross the waiting-room, still walking quickly.

Her shoes struck the floor of the passage.

Laura did not move.

Then she heard her mother's voice. 'Oh, goodness. Charlotte, wait. Wait a second. Oh, what a mercy . . . Just stay there a second.'

Laura opened the door and went out. She said, 'Mother, you don't mean to say you've left the trap open again?'

'It's all right,' said Mrs. Swanton with guilty cheerfulness. 'I remembered. I was just on my way back. No harm done.'

'Another few seconds,' said Laura, 'and it wouldn't have been all right. It would have been too late.'

The flap went down with a bang. Laura and Charlotte walked across it and on into the kitchen.

Now Laura knew. Now she could evade it no longer. Somehow, in the time of waiting for Peter to come home, she was going to get rid of Charlotte. It was no good shirking the full awareness of her intentions.

She intended Charlotte to die.

5

The school secretary knocked and went into the study.

Mr. Cartwright, interrupted in the course of a carefully developed sentence which had reached its second parenthetical clause — 'a state of affairs which, I fear, our County Council wilfully ignores, the Education Committee sidesteps, and my Governors are unwilling to face, to the detriment of the children's welfare' — cleared his throat very deliberately and turned his back on her.

Miss Jones, too, cleared her throat. She smiled apologetically at the visiting H.M.I., who was in point of fact glad of the respite. He had been subjected to a long lecture on Mr. Cartwright's need of money if the school was not to fall down, and the need for more plasticity on the part of those authorities who dealt with building allocations and the provision of teaching materials. Plasticity . . . 'And there's another word,' Mr. Cartwright had said, 'on the tip of my tongue.' But then he had seen a piece of chalk on the window ledge, and it had prompted him to mention that even chalk was in short supply, thanks to the miserliness of the Education Committee, who most unhelpfully accused him of having spent all his allocation for the coming year.

Recognising the phrases which she had caught on opening the door, Miss Jones knew that the headmaster had a lot more to say yet. She was sorry for the H.M.I., and sorry, too, for the staff, whose shortcomings would soon be summed up by Mr. Cartwright before the inspector was allowed to enter their classrooms.

She said: 'I'm sorry to break in, but — '

'I'm very busy, Miss Jones.'

His voice was sweetly reasonable. During her first year at the school she had been several times reduced to tears by that sweet, magisterially infallible voice; but now it had not the same power over her. Sometimes it provoked a mild nausea, but generally speaking she was immune. She ignored the gentle menace in his tone now, and said:

'It's rather important. Gilbert Drysdale's grandfather.'

'Later, I think, Miss Jones.'

'I've had a telephone call to say that he has been taken suddenly ill again.'

Mr. Cartwright sighed. He looked away from Miss Jones, through the window and across the school field. His attention was distracted by the sight of a master walking across the grass.

'You might give my compliments to Mr. Smethwick,' he said, 'and ask him to study Item — er — ten of the School Regulations. I mentioned this business of wearing a diagonal path across the field only the other morning at prayers. If the staff can't set a good example . . . ' He shrugged despairingly, as one whose load had been rendered just that much too heavy, and then turned back to the inspector. 'Now, where were we?'

'Mr. Drysdale is ill,' said Miss Jones.

He did not spare her a glance, but said distantly: 'The old man is always having these bouts.'

'This time they say — '

'Surely you can cope, Miss Jones?'

'Yes, I can cope.'

She went out. She could go and find Gilbert Drysdale and send him home — and then, later in the day, that deceptively retentive memory would purr into wakefulness, and Mr. Cartwright would ask what had been done about the boy. She would tell him. And the long arms would scoop up the sleeves of his gown, would be raised imploringly towards her. 'But the boy shouldn't have gone without seeing me first. You know I make it an absolute rule that no child must leave the school without first seeing the headmaster. The headmaster is responsible to the parents ... ' Yes, already she could hear the reproaches. And then, if she were to reply 'But you told me ... ' there would come the sincere, puzzled frown. '*I* told you, Miss Jones? I'm sure I gave no instructions that the boy should be allowed to go.' He would wait, triumphant. Of course he had given no instructions. He had committed himself to nothing definite: it was not in his nature to do so. If she were to refuse to be defeated, and continue pressing him — 'Did you mean, then, that the boy should *not* have gone home when his grandfather was ill?' — the virtuous puzzlement would shade into reproach. No answer would be forthcoming; only a sad shaking of that impressive head. Of course nothing of that sort had been said either.

Miss Jones came to a halt in the corridor, breathing hard. She must not allow herself to become neurotic. She must not take things to heart. She was getting as bad as some of the older members of the staff-room.

Where would Gilbert Drysdale be at this time of day?

She knew nearly all the form periods off by heart, and after a moment's hesitation she went towards the biology lab.

There was no doubt that the sensible thing to do was to tell the master in charge of the class that Gil was to go home. The sensible, human, reasonable thing. Let him get off at once to his grandfather, and when Mr. Cartwright's

blandly evasive disapproval was mani-
fested, argue it out with him point by
point.

But why should *she* have to bear the
brunt of it: why should she have to face
that sly, derogatory inquisition and the
subsequent pontifications? A fit of rebel-
lion came upon her. This time the game
would be played strictly according to the
rules, and he could carry the consequences.

After all, there couldn't really be much
wrong with old Mr. Drysdale. He was
always having these spells — the headmaster was right in that respect — and it
would do Gilbert no harm to wait.

She went into the lab, and emerged a
minute later with Gilbert. They went
together towards the study, but on the
corner near her office she stopped.

'He's got someone with him,' she said,
'but he shouldn't be long. I've told him
your grandfather isn't well. But he'd like
to see you before you go home. Just sit on
the chair outside the door.'

She stood on the corner until he had
settled on the chair, and then she went

back to her office to type out the second of the day's circulars to the staff about current misdemeanours in the cloakroom supervision.

Gil listened to the buzz of voices from a nearby classroom. He moved restlessly. He longed to be on his way home. There had been similar messages before, but he had never got used to them. Each time, he had wanted to dash out of the building and get on his bike and get moving. Waiting to see the Head was a waste of time. Yet at the same time he wanted, in a way, to see old Cartwright: he wanted him to come out and say something reassuring in that smarmy deep voice of his. They all imitated that voice and knew it was 'put on', and rarely paid any attention to what it said; but there was something nice about having it directed at you, at you personally, when you weren't feeling too good.

Mr. Cartwright remained within his room.

Ten minutes went by. Another five, and the bell would go for next lesson.

Four or five times before, Gil had had

this choking feeling. It seemed worse today. His grandfather might be really ill this time . . . might not be able to do a thing for himself . . . might be calling out . . . might die before he, Gil, got home.

The door of the study opened. Mr. Cartwright, talking in an insistent sort of way, came out with another man.

Gil said: 'Sir.'

'Come and see me at break time,' said the headmaster without pausing.

'But I was told — Miss Jones said — it's about my grandfather, sir.'

Mr. Cartwright blinked. He looked for one instant as though he were about to make some effort to understand, then he glanced at his companion, looked beyond him up the corridor, and said testily: 'Break time is the time to come and see the headmaster.'

It was like drawing a line under the answer of a sum, thought Gil queerly; and at the back of his mind a remoter self was aware that he was playing with similes again. He thought confusedly of Charlotte; then tried not to think of her. He stared after the headmaster, who was walking away, deep in conversation.

He felt strange, lonely, cheated.

Like drawing a line under a sum, that's what it was: you drew the line and that was the end and you could forget about it and go on to the next thing.

Some people could.

He went along to the cloakroom. He had a sudden urgent need to go to the lavatory.

Afterwards, weak inside, he went out to the shed, dragged his bike out from the tangle of tilted machinery, and rode home.

His grandfather was dead. He was too late.

6

Mrs. Swanton made all the funeral arrangements.

'It's the least we can do,' she said.

She worked with a controlled fury that was utterly unlike her. It was only on the morning of the funeral day that her legs gave out and she had to sit down, staring at something which nobody else could see.

Charlotte felt cold. She seemed to hear within herself an echo of what was going on in Mrs. Swanton's mind. Mrs. Drysdale had been a school friend of hers, and was dead; and now Drysdale, too, had gone. Mrs. Swanton had taken on the burden of the arrangements for this day, had taken Gilbert back into the Swanton house, had seen the solicitor — all in order to stop herself thinking, to stop herself turning round and looking for her contemporaries and finding they were fewer and fewer . . . even, perhaps, that there were none of them left.

It would be all right in a few days. Mrs. Swanton was not old, and, as Laura curtly informed her, she was in perfectly good health. But for the moment she was acutely conscious of the shadow that had crept closer. It might, once this day was over, recede; but it would come again, it would edge nearer, until it was fully upon her.

'Unfortunate,' was Laura's comment on Mr. Drysdale's unexpected death.

Laura was annoyed. Someone had died who ought not to have died, and that put her in a bad temper. 'One chance in a thousand,' she said. 'One in ten thousand. A fluke.' While Mrs. Swanton was making preparations and saying over and over again, 'Well, I'll see it's all done properly — it'll be done the way Lucy would have wanted it,' and one of her well-meaning friends was bobbing in and out with such condolences as 'We all have to come to it . . . he did look after that boy, he did his best, poor old dear . . . at any rate it was quick, it's best that way, I hope I go like that,' Laura was explaining to anyone who would listen that it was not a thing any doctor would have expected to happen. The tying and injecting had been expertly done, the leg was coming along excellently . . . and then a clot had flown off and gone to the lung. It had been quick. Mr. Drysdale had been talking to the milkman when it happened. He had stopped talking, muttered something, tried to turn round as though to look for something in the house, coughed up blood, and died.

'Of course there's always the *risk*,' said Laura to Charlotte, using Charlotte, as before, merely as an audience. 'But no one would have predicted it.'

Charlotte listened without taking in the sense of what was being said. She wished she could have gone to Gil and comforted him — talked to him, listened to him, or just sat with him. But Mrs. Swanton was the only one who could go near him.

For Gil the funeral was huge and terrifying. It was a dreadful thing that caught him up and thrust him along. He could not catch hold of the familiar everyday things and cling to them.

Something inexorable dragged people into the house, drove them up to the church and the cemetery, and at last allowed them to disperse.

He was surrounded, yet alone. People around him were kind: they acted as a buffer, encircling him and facing outwards, staving off worry, trying to insulate him. But they were strangers. He was horribly separate from them all. In a way it might have been better if he had not been so well protected; if he had been allowed to assert that this whole business involved himself and his grandfather and nobody else (except perhaps God? — he was shy of thinking of that). But he could not bring himself to protest.

He had always known that this day must come. Grandfather must die. But now that it had come and he had been forced to accept it, he felt sick and empty. Somehow, in his imagination, this day was to have been final. His grandfather's death was to have been the end. He had never tried to visualise what might lie beyond. Now, here he was, still alive: he would go on living, and he had never thought about that until now.

'Of course, there's no point in keeping the house,' Mrs. Swanton said to him. 'You can't live there on your own.'

'I want it,' he said numbly.

As might have been expected, Doctor Swanton wasted no time. She asked the obvious, unanswerable question: 'And the rent? Where will that come from?'

He shook his head in misery.

'You couldn't manage there without anyone to look after you, Gilbert,' said Mrs. Swanton soothingly.

It had always been a shabby little house and he had never loved it. He had admired the Swanton house, and once — how long ago it was ! — he had thought of what Doctor Swanton had suggested to him about living here if . . . oh, *if* a lot of things . . .

Now he felt that he could not bear to leave the house. It must be preserved just as it was. The yellowed photographs, the out-of-date calendars, and all the bits and pieces his grandfather had accumulated must stay where they were. If the house were no longer his, there would be no shelter; no home.

'Still,' Mrs. Swanton was saying, 'there's no need to go into all that now. In a few days' time — '

'I think it's as well to get these things settled,' said Doctor Swanton.

'I expect we can sell the furniture to someone — '

'No,' said Gilbert.

'But Gilbert, if you come to live here, there won't be room for it all. You can bring one or two things you particularly want to keep, and the money you get for the rest will come in very useful.'

To come and live here . . .

Doctor Swanton was staring at him. 'Well?' she said in a stiff sort of voice. 'Do you want to come here — for good?'

She seemed to think it was terribly important. To Gil, it was not a choice at all. He knew they were right: he could not keep the house and he could not keep all the furniture.

He would come here because there was nowhere else to go. He had nobody else in the world now but these people.

7

Charlotte got off the bus at Tapton Harbour.

The driver and conductor were the only other two on the bus. They climbed down and went to sit outside the pub, sprawling on the bench and looking out over the golden pebbles that made the ranges a blur of evening brilliance.

Charlotte went to the river bank and looked across. Walter was on his way towards the ferry from the other side. He waved to her, and she waved back.

Behind her the driver and conductor laughed, but when she looked round they were staring at the bus. It would stand here, at the end of its run, for ten minutes before going back.

She watched Walter as he was rowed across by the ferryman. It made her feel rather foolish, standing there and smiling, while he grinned back, the two of them not liking to shout to one another across the water.

Then he was scrambling up the green-slimed ladder to the bank. He put his hand possessively on her arm.

'Hello, Lottie.'

His friends, he had told her last time, called him Wally. She said : 'Hello, Walter.'

This evening he was wearing an open-necked shirt, green sports coat, and flannels. It was the first time he had worn civilian clothes instead of his uniform, and Charlotte was not sure that she liked the change. He looked so trim and appealingly cocky in his uniform; now he was rather cheap, in some way she could not define.

'Let's get off the road,' he said.

His fingers were warm on her arm. This evening he was quite sure of himself. He had arranged to meet her here, she had come, and the rest of the programme was clearly mapped out in his head.

They went past the bus and turned down a sandy path between two houses. Beyond lay a stretch of fine shingle and then the rough, sparse grass leading to the deep hollows in which sea water was collected and diverted after each high tide.

They would be sheltered there, out of sight.

Walter was trying to make her walk quickly. Charlotte held back. She had come willingly, with an excitement that matched his own, but now there was something disheartening about the hard brightness of the shingle ahead, and the desolate plain beyond it. She was aware of Walter glancing at her thin yellow frock and her bare legs.

She glanced back. The bus had not yet left.

'Just a minute,' she said abruptly.

'What's up?'

Gilbert had appeared at the mouth of the gap through which they had just come. He looked back over his shoulder, then leaned on an uneven length of fencing in front of one of the houses.

He had been down, she guessed at once, for a last look at his old home. Or perhaps not a last look. Perhaps he would come again, reminding himself, trying to hold on to that which he ought to relinquish.

She uttered an exclamation that was like a sob.

'What *is* it?' demanded Walter petulantly.

She pulled herself suddenly free, and began to walk towards Gil.

Walter was startled. She had gone a few yards before he began to follow her, trotting after her.

'Hey . . . what the hell?'

Gil heard the sound, and turned his head slowly.

Charlotte called : 'Hello, Gil.'

His expression was like a slap across her face. It seemed to reach out, to insult her. There was such undisguised loathing in it that she faltered.

A hand was on her arm again.

'Look here, what's going on?'

'I'm sorry, Walter, I must just speak to him. I can't — '

'Doesn't look as though he's keen on it,' said Walter. 'Come on — we haven't got all night. More's the pity,' he added with a harsh attempt at jocularity.

'I won't be a minute.'

His fingers were digging into her

forearm. Her flesh seemed to shrink from him. She saw Gil staring, his mouth twisted.

Then she broke loose and began to run towards him. He disappeared, and on the other side of the houses she heard the bus beginning to thud rhythmically.

'Lottie!'

She caught up with Gil by the two steps up into the bus. There was no one inside but the conductor. Gil jumped in, not pausing. Charlotte turned on the step as the bus began to move. Walter's upturned face was ludicrous. He was shouting something, but she could not hear a word. She tried to shout back — 'Sorry, I'll explain later, it's all right.'

She did not know how she would explain. She was not at all sure that she could, and not sure that it would be all right.

Gilbert went to the front seat and sat down in the middle of it, taking up so much room that she could not sit beside him. She staggered as the bus turned the corner on to the main road away from Tapton Harbour, and sank into the seat on the other side of the aisle.

Gilbert stared straight ahead at the back of the driver's neck.

Charlotte said: 'I didn't know you'd be down here this evening, Gil. We could have come down together.'

It was a silly remark. He did not make a move.

She tried again. 'It's nice to have you back in the house. I do hope . . . '

But what was the good of trying to tell him what she hoped? He was not prepared to listen. His profile was set and unyielding. The two of them sat right up at the front of the bus, and there was a greater emptiness between them than in all the unoccupied seats behind them.

The conductor came along, grinning to himself. Charlotte took out enough money for two fares, but by the time she had it in her hand she saw that Gilbert was holding out a return.

She remembered that she, too, had bought a return, and that before descending from the bus on the journey down she had crumpled it up and thrown it away.

If the conductor remembered that, he

did not give any sign. He took the money from her, smirking into her face, and gave her a single ticket. When he had gone away again, the space between Charlotte and Gilbert seemed wider than before.

They finished the journey in silence. At Brookchurch they got off and walked side by side to the front door of the house, without exchanging a word. Indoors, Gilbert left her at once.

★   ★   ★

Three days later Charlotte said that she had had a letter from Peter and that he wanted to see her after all. She would make the journey to the North.

At the end of a week she had still not returned.

8

Charlotte had escaped. And though Laura hated the sight of her, that had not been the idea at all.

'The poor child must be feeling upset,' said Mrs. Swanton. 'I expect seeing her husband upset her, and she needs a day or two on her own to get over it.' She said 'her husband' with impersonal sympathy, as though she had forgotten that the man in question was her own son Peter. 'She's probably staying up there a night or two — '

'I don't believe she ever went there,' said Laura.

'What? Oh, really, Laura. I don't know what's got into you.'

'I'm sure there wasn't any letter for her that day. Did you see one?'

'Well — '

'Did you see her reading one?'

'I don't see why she should make up a fib like that. She just wants to stay there

— or perhaps in London, on the way back
. . . that's it, she's staying with friends in
London.'

'I can imagine what sort of friends,'
said Laura.

'We mustn't worry. We must just leave
her to work things out in her own way.
It's *her* life.'

'And Peter's,' said Laura.

'I don't see what harm she can do
Peter,' said Mrs. Swanton. 'I mean,' she
added vaguely, 'Peter's safe enough where
he is.'

Laura left her, and went into the
consulting-room. She put in a trunk call
to the Governor of the prison, and drew
symmetrical patterns on the blotter while
she waited — a rectangle with bars down
it, and a vertical figure that might have
been made up of two gallows trees
touching, the ropes dangling.

When the call came through she was
told that the Governor was busy and
could not speak to her. By making several
brusque, unspecific remarks about her
status as a doctor, and hinting at urgent
medical reasons, she at last got in touch

with him. He was not anxious to answer her questions. But in the end she had established the fact that Peter had not been visited by his wife. They knew nothing about his wife.

Laura reported this with cold triumph to her mother.

'It's none of our business,' said Mrs. Swanton defensively. It was clear that if Laura had not been so persistent, Mrs. Swanton herself would have been the first to worry and make frightened guesses at what had happened. As it was, she felt herself bound to speak up for Charlotte. 'She'll be back in a day or two.'

The day or two passed, became three days, and Charlotte did not return to Brookchurch.

Laura telephoned Doctor Whiting in Jury. With his usual infuriating affability he agreed to take any urgent calls for her next day. Laura worked until eleven o'clock that night, making routine visits for the next two days, leaving as little as possible for Doctor Whiting. The following morning she went up to town on the early train. It was her first trip to London since she had gone up to Peter's trial — that day on which she had first met Charlotte.

Charlotte would be in London. She was one of those people who belonged in London; and, Laura was convinced, she was also one of those who would move in a limited area, within a certain circle of friends and places.

She had to be brought back. Laura was clear and decisive now. Her original uncertainties had been dispelled.

From now on she was consciously, deliberately the hunter. When the moment came to strike, she would recognise it — and act. There must be no trace; she must not, in striking, expose herself to danger. For Peter's sake as much as her own, there must be no scandal.

Perhaps she would find it possible to set a trap, or perhaps the opportunity would present itself unexpectedly. She must be ready.

'I can't think what you're hoping to do,' Mrs. Swanton said. 'You oughtn't to pester the poor child. She'll come and see us again when she's ready.'

Laura ignored her. She set off in the haze of the summer morning and sat quite still in the compartment as the fields rose to the tunnelled ridges and gave way at last to groves of chimneys and the deeper haze of the city. She did not read, and was not consciously making any plans.

She went first to the house in which she had met Charlotte.

Charlotte had not been there. There had not been any word from her since she had sent money and instructions for the removal of her personal belongings — and a fine nuisance that had been, you'd have thought the least she could do was come and sort it out herself; still, she was always a pleasant girl and no doubt there were good reasons . . .

Decisions must have been shaping themselves for Laura as she travelled up. She went straight from the flat to the nearest telephone box and took up the last volume of the telephone directory.

The echoes were remarkably clear. Trivial things came back to her when she needed them. She could hear Charlotte in one of her reminiscent moods, giggling over some disjointed story. 'As Harry Watford used to say . . . I'll never forget Janie and Bossy Merriman . . . that time we were out with the Watfords . . . ' The name of Watford had come back over and over again, reverberating with remembered amusement. Those, for Charlotte, had been the days. 'Harry Watford, he really was the limit, you've no idea . . . '

Laura found four Watfords, Henry, in the directory, and one Watford, H. W., two of them in the W.2 district. She lifted the receiver.

Then she paused.

If the wife — the Watfords, she recalled, were often referred to in the plural — were at home, and knew anything about Charlotte, would she be prepared to answer questions over the phone? A voice in a receiver could be very uncommunicative : Laura would learn nothing that the speaker did not wish to pass on. Diagnosis from a series of vibrations in a metal diaphragm was difficult.

She put the receiver back in its cradle,

noted the two addresses, and left the telephone box.

She went to the nearer address. The morning was racing by : she realised that she had very little time and that her quest could so easily be a hopeless one.

London was said to be the finest place in the world for anyone who wished to lose himself, or herself.

Nevertheless she was still sure that Charlotte would not plunge into a completely unknown part of the city. She would not have the courage to cut herself away from the places she had known. Desperation might have driven her back to London, but it would not drive her into an utterly new existence.

Desperation . . . Why was she desperate?

Laura had several theories. She would find out, in all probability, which was the right one. If she had time, that was, before . . . before the end.

The house to which she came now was a small one with a flat roof, incongruously sandwiched between two taller ones. It had almost certainly not been painted since before the war.

The woman who opened the door was about Laura's own age, but there was little resemblance between them. Her features were slack and puffy, but it could be seen that she had once been very attractive. If her caller this morning had been a man, she would, Laura sensed, have produced a smile that was still charming — the easy, responsive, still achingly youthful smile of a woman used to the company and jokes and advances of men.

As it was, the face was impassive. The woman waited for Laura to identify herself.

Laura said : 'Mrs. Watford?'

'Yes.' There was a trace of reluctance in the reply.

'I'm Doctor Swanton.'

'I haven't sent for a doctor. Don't need one. At least' — she squeaked with unexpectedly skittish laughter — 'I don't think I do.'

'I believe you knew my brother, Peter Swanton.'

'Peter?' Mrs. Watford stared. Then she

smiled. 'Oh, *him*. Charlie's husband.'

'I'm looking for Charlotte,' said Laura quickly.

'You won't find her here, my pet.'

'I rather hoped you would be able to help me.' Laura was furious that she should be kept standing on the step like this, but she tried not to show it. 'I'm worried about her.'

'She'll be all right.'

'You know where she is, then?'

'Me? Why should I know, my dear?'

Laura said with terrible patience: 'She has been staying with us, and now she's disappeared. We're afraid she may — may not be well. I've come up to town to try and find her. She ought not to be wandering about on her own.'

Mrs. Watford scratched her head. She looked uncertain : her character was as blowsy and unkempt as her appearance. Laura tensed. Here was a woman who could be easily swayed. It was a matter of approach, of applying the right pressure, carefully, at the right moment.

Mrs. Watford said: 'You mean she's . . . there's anything the matter with her?'

'Of course not,' said Laura brightly. 'That would be a most misleading way of putting it.'

The door was opened wider. Laura went in, and followed Mrs. Watford down a narrow passage. A Hogarth print hung askew on one wall. A low bookshelf jutted out at the end, as they went into the room beyond.

There were two low tables in the middle of the room — the sort of tables that required one to sprawl languidly, half on the floor, if one proposed to make use of them. Several empty glasses with red stains in the bottom were clustering on each table and also on the top of a radio in one corner. A smell of smoke and drink was trapped in the gaudy chequered curtains. Over the fireplace was a long picture in a yellow frame; the picture was composed of squares and blobs. It reminded Laura of something virulent seen under a microscope.

Mrs. Watford nodded her towards a chair. Laura sank down into it. The chair was just too low for one to be able to get up again without an effort.

'Of course,' said Mrs. Watford, 'that business of Peter shook her up. You could tell that.' She blinked at a group of glasses near her elbow. 'Care for a drink?'

'Thank you, no.'

'No.' Mrs. Watford looked momentarily sad. 'I suppose it is a bit too early.'

Laura said: 'Have you seen Charlotte recently?'

'Last night,' said Mrs. Watford, snapping the words out quickly before she could change her mind.

'Where?'

'At a friend's.'

There was something in her tone that convinced Laura she was already beginning to hedge again.

Laura said: 'Do I know the friend? If you could give me the address . . . '

'Oh, hell,' said Mrs. Watford. 'Actually it was a pub. The one we always go to. The one Charlie's always been to.'

'And after you'd been to the pub — what then?'

'We came home earlyish,' said Mrs. Watford plaintively, slumping back in resentment from this cross-examination.

'We had a party fixed up here.'

'Charlotte came with you?'

'She said she wasn't in the mood. I thought then that she looked a bit queer. Not concentrating at all, if you know what I mean.'

'I know exactly what you mean,' said Laura quickly, with sinister emphasis.

'Oh, dear,' said Mrs. Watford. 'Poor kid.'

'It would be better,' said Laura, 'if I could find her in time. It's not advisable for her to be alone.'

'She wasn't alone. She was with a man.'

With a man. Laura felt a tremor of disgust.

'Not that I'm saying anything,' Mrs. Watford rushed on. 'She never was one of *those* . . . I mean, she didn't look as though she was enjoying herself.' She wriggled uncomfortably, not sure what she was talking about.

Laura said : 'Where can I find her?'

'You might look' — Mrs. Watford was looking away at a thick unsymmetrical vase, as though to dissociate herself from the information she was allowing to come out — 'in the Malt Shovel, in Beckonbridge Grove. That's where we saw her yesterday. She and Peter always used to drift in and out of there. Not that she would ever go in on her own. We used to laugh at her for being shy about going into a pub. She's a queer little thing.'

Mrs. Watford looked around the room again and showed signs of wanting to wipe her eyes. It was impossible to tell whether the sight of so many empty glasses had affected her, or whether she was melancholy over the thought of queer little Charlotte.

'Thank you,' said Laura.

The woman got up thankfully, eager to be rid of her. A suspicion struck Laura. She said :

'That's the only lead you can give? You can't be more definite — you've no idea where she's staying?'

''Fraid not. I'd no notion she was . . . that people were looking for her. Harry said afterwards that she looked a bit odd, but then it was ages since we'd seen her. And it was none of our business.'

Laura left the house. She thought that she might well have been staved off with half-truths, but at least the woman had seemed honest in her information about the public house. It was only to be hoped that Charlotte did not see the Watfords or telephone them before Laura could get to her.

She found the Malt Shovel and waited for a long time in the saloon bar, perched on a stool near the counter so that she could look through a doorway behind the bar into the public bar as well.

Charlotte did not come.

Little groups of young men with beards and warm-smelling corduroys gathered behind her, and drew in a number of young women with shrill voices. An elderly man clutching a violin case held court in what was evidently his accustomed corner.

Laura could clearly visualise Charlotte among such people. She so obviously belonged here that one expected the door to open any second and admit her. But it did not.

Laura had a makeshift lunch at the bar,

indifferently selecting a slab of meat pie, potato salad, pickled walnuts and cold spaghetti. When she had finished, Charlotte had not arrived, and it was almost closing time.

Laura asked the barman whether Mrs. Swanton was expected. The name meant nothing to him, but as she spoke she detected a tension in one of the groups further down the room. Their loud argument became suddenly softer, and she had the impression that they were listening without turning their heads towards her. She glanced hopefully at them. Their faces were averted. Clustering together, they looked blank and unyielding.

At closing time they all shuffled or sauntered out into the afternoon streets. The sun shone. A dark cloud over a nearby church threatened rain.

The end of Beckonbridge Grove tilted down into a grey road lined with grey houses and a few shops. A tattered cinema poster made the only splash of colour, and that colour was rapidly fading.

Laura had an overwhelming sensation of vast, empty spaces — emptier than the marshes she knew so well. She could walk for miles and not find the one person she sought. And if she did find her, what then? To kill her now, here, in London, was impracticable. She had spoken to too many people about Charlotte now. If Charlotte died, Laura Swanton would be the first person they would look for.

Unless, of course, she could find Charlotte on her own, and then continue the search, expressing horror when the news of Charlotte's death reached her.

How was it to be done?

In the first place, how to find Charlotte?

The remaining hours of the afternoon blurred into one another. Laura went purposelessly back to the square in which Charlotte's home had been, then wandered on through streets that led from nowhere to nowhere. Hatred dazed her faculties. She turned right at a corner, and right again. Somewhere in the neighbourhood, somewhere within this erratic path she was tracing, Charlotte would almost certainly be. She might walk out of a house at any moment. She might be buying bread at that confectioner's on the other side of the road; might be ready to get off that bus that was thrusting its red bulk in to the curb through the traffic; might be lying on a bed in one of those gaunt houses, staring at the ceiling.

What was she doing about money? Laura had doled out a weekly allowance to her while she was in Brookchurch, but Charlotte was not the sort to save. She would hardly have put it away regularly, accumulating enough to escape. Why come to Brookchurch in the first place, if she had wanted to be in London; or why, having got there and found it not to her liking, not simply make sensible, adult arrangements to leave? To get a job somewhere, to shake hands and say goodbye . . .

Laura swayed on the edge of a pavement. Traffic swished in close to her, accelerated, and went off at a tangent. She closed her eyes, felt that she would fall forward, and opened them again.

Now she understood how murderers came to make mistakes. She realised how clouded the judgment could become by the intensity of one's hatred. Minor details became exasperating. The incessant wrangling in the head began to scream into incoherence, until there was nothing but a babel of loathing, viciousness, and the longing to put an end to it — the longing that could only be fulfilled by action, silencing the clamour at last. One would rush blindly on, yearning only for the peace that would come with accomplishment; and that was when the mistakes would be made.

She felt purposeful but unfocussed. Inside her was a frightening concentration of energy that could not be released until the right time. The pressure was intolerable.

Yet until she found Charlotte it all meant nothing. She was venomous yet harmless, at this moment. The longing in her mind was like a deadly poison stowed away in a cupboard — harmless until it found a substance to attack.

At the end of the afternoon she turned

back towards the Malt Shovel, simply because there was nowhere else she could look.

She had forgotten Peter. She wanted only Charlotte. When Charlotte was out of the way, she would be able to think again of Peter and the way she would look after him when he was free. He would come home. This time she would make sure that he did not want to leave again. She would make up to Peter for all that he had suffered: for all his mistakes and his misery.

The last possible train home would leave at eight o'clock. She looked at the clock over the bar every two or three minutes, and turned towards the door each time it opened.

Charlotte came in a few minutes before seven o'clock.

9

She stood outside the familiar doors and tried to pluck up the courage to enter. Or, rather, not so much the courage as the inclination. She was listless. To do anything whatever called for more effort than she was capable of. She felt drawn towards the comfort of the saloon bar in which she had talked and laughed so often; but at the same time she felt that it would solve nothing, offer no consolation.

Charlotte went slowly past the door and walked fifty yards down the road.

She was a foreigner here now. Once you had taken up your roots from London, the hard streets closed over the place where you had been. Her friends, she sensed, had been vaguely embarrassed by her. To drop out of a circle such as she had known was to lose all contact: coming back, you found that the topics of conversation had changed, the friends had made new friends, and the old ease of companionship had gone.

That freedom which she had associated with life in London was a terrifying freedom. Nobody cared, nobody remained faithful. Freedom here was loneliness.

She had very little money left. She had started out with little, and would not have managed to survive even this long without her friends. Friends who were no longer friends.

That job she had meant to get . . . She had done nothing about it. Her job was being Peter's wife. She was good at that. She was good at nothing else.

Charlotte went another ten paces to a road junction, and looked down to her left. Down there by the traffic lights was another pub. It was completely alien. She could not go in there. There were so few places she could go. To eat in the places where she had eaten with Peter, or to go to the cinemas they had frequented, was to spend money. When the money was spent and the time used up, there was still no end: still there would be tomorrow and the next day, and so many more days until Peter came out and gave her a purpose in life. When Peter was there, looking after her yet dependent on her, she could deal with things : she was not afraid.

She turned and went back to the Malt Shovel, and went into the saloon bar, not seeing anyone until she was right inside and close to the bar.

Then she saw Laura.

Laura said : 'I wondered if you would come.'

The door was a long way behind. To turn and run into the street was just possible. Only just. No ; not possible at all.

Suddenly she was overwhelmed by a feeling of relief. Laura was real. It was no good running away. Laura was the answer: Laura and Brookchurch and Mrs. Swanton were the answers to all the questions, as they had been once before.

Charlotte approached her, looking into Laura's eyes.

'Will you have something to drink?' asked Laura.

'Yes, please.'

'We'll have to hurry. The last train goes at eight.'

'I shall have to get my things.'

'Where are they?'

'At a friend's,' said Charlotte. 'Not far from here.'

'What will you have to drink, then?'

'A gin and French, please.'

'And then we must go,' said Laura.

'Yes.'

She took up the glass that was set before her, and drank. Laura gazed at her. There was nothing in her face to show what she was feeling; yet Charlotte's instinctive relief at seeing her began to ebb. She did not want to go back to Brookchurch. And yet . . .

'Are you ready?' said Laura.

There was some gin left in the glass. Charlotte sipped it, reluctant to finish and then have to begin the journey back to that house on the marsh.

From the corner there was a warm, soothing buzz of voices. She recognised one of the artists who used to sit with her and Peter and curse the Royal Academy at the top of his voice.

He caught her eye, grinned, and looked quickly away.

Help, she absurdly thought at him. Do please help me. Don't let this woman take me away. She's a witch. I shan't live to see Peter ever again.

Please, please do something. Don't let me walk out of this place.

She whispered: 'How did you find me?'

'I didn't think you'd be far from here,' said Laura. 'I came up this morning — '

'This morning?'

It had taken only a day to find her. Laura was a witch.

I must be drunk, thought Charlotte. No, I'm not. I wish I were drunk.

Laura's eyes did not waver. She continued to look at Charlotte with complete certainty. Laura knew everything there was to know. She always knew what to do.

'We must be off,' said Laura.

'Yes,' said Charlotte.

She finished her drink. The men in the corner did not look up as the two women went out.

'This friend of yours,' said Laura in the bleak indifference of the street: 'where does she live?'

Charlotte said : 'Over there and along on the right-hand side.' And she added: 'It's not a she. It's a man.'

'I see,' said Laura.

'No. No, you don't see. You're quite wrong. Nothing like that at all. Just somebody we used to know — Peter and I — an awfully kind man, and I've been such a nuisance to him.'

In the train she was still protesting in fits and starts. There was no reason why she should make excuses to Laura; but those accusing eyes drew explanations from her, as though it were essential to save herself . . .

She put her hand over her eyes, pressing against her brow. She squeezed hard, trying to squeeze her thoughts into silence and to stop worrying.

'Headache?' said Laura.

'Yes.'

Laura patted her pockets, then looked in her handbag.

'Here. Take three of these. They're only the usual mild things, but they'll help.'

'I haven't got a drink of water.'

'Chew them,' said Laura, sounding her

usual self. 'They go down just as well that way.'

Charlotte bit into the first, and made a face. Then she put the other two into her mouth and crunched them up. Bitterness seemed to dry up her tongue and pull in the roof of her mouth.

'How awful,' she said.

They were alone in the compartment. Evening sunshine lay along the roofs of houses and plunged into the wells of blocks of flats. A cinema neon sign shone palely in the distance. Streets swooped at intervals under railway bridges, and Charlotte looked down on buses that quivered and were gone.

She said : 'This man I've been with — '

'There's no need to tell me about it,' said Laura. 'It doesn't make any difference.'

'But it does. You've got the wrong idea altogether.'

Station platforms streamed loudly past. An electric train moved away on a parallel line, swung gently in, and came sneaking up outside the window.

'You see,' said Charlotte, desperate and truthful, 'he's . . . well, he's not interested in women. He's . . . one of *those*. You know. But he's so awfully kind. We always liked him.'

'It doesn't make any difference,' said Laura again.

'How can you say that, Laura? I mean, I was only staying there until I found something to do.'

The electric train drew level with them, and then fell away again as another suburban station claimed its attention.

Laura was staring out of the window. She had chosen a seat with her back to the engine, and so was able to watch the lunges and recessions of the rival train. She said:

'What sort of thing were you looking for? What sort of job?'

'I hadn't really thought. I was waiting to see what was best.'

'This is best,' said Laura.

They plunged into a short tunnel, and when they emerged there was a low green embankment on each side, with only an occasional roof or chimney visible over it, through clustering trees.

Laura leaned forward and put her hand

on the catch of the outer door. Not far behind, the electric train let out its throaty hoot.

The train they were on was slowing slightly.

Charlotte said : 'Don't fiddle with the door, Laura.' She felt drowsy. Her headache was gone, or going. As it went, tiredness closed gently down on her. 'The door's all right,' she muttered. 'I know. I tested it when I got in — didn't you notice? I always do try doors.'

'Do you?'

'I've always had a silly fear of leaning on a door, or falling against it, and being thrown out.'

'Have you?'

'Often had dreams about it,' said Charlotte sluggishly.

Laura's hand was still on the door, but she was looking up at Charlotte. Her eyes were wide. Once, and once only, she made an abrupt movement with her head: she glanced from Charlotte to the door and back again, as though measuring the distance.

Charlotte felt the dream fear suddenly

upon her. She saw the familiar vision of the open door and felt herself being sucked out. That was one of the recurrent dreams : being pulled down from a tower, toppling from a bridge, or being drawn out of a railway carriage door.

'Oh, everybody dreams that sort of thing,' Peter had easily said. 'With me, it's falling under tube trains.'

Everybody dreamed that sort of thing. But not everybody had it become real before their eyes. Not everybody saw the door actually beginning to open — just an inch, so that cold air came streaming into the compartment.

She said : 'No, Laura. Laura, you can't.'

'Can't what?' said Laura blandly.

The sound of the electric train crept up once more, a high steady whining that pierced through the drumming of their own train.

'Laura . . . '

Charlotte stood up. The train lurched, and she swayed to and fro for a moment, dizzy, feeling the draught striking up at her face, seeing Laura leaning towards her.

Then the corridor door slid back suddenly, and the inspector said :

'Tickets, please.'

Laura drew the door shut with a bang, and sank back into her seat.

'That was a near thing,' she said breathlessly.

'Having trouble, madam?'

Laura said: 'The door started to come open. I got to it only just in time.'

Charlotte staggered towards the corridor side of the compartment, and sank into the corner seat. The inspector went over to the door and tested it.

'Seems all right now. Lucky you spotted it.'

He checked their tickets and then went out. The corridor door slid shut. On the other side, the electric train loomed up once more, with passengers peering curiously from their world into this one. For a few seconds the two speeds matched, and between the trains there was apparent stillness. Then the green coaches abruptly swung away down another line.

Charlotte could not look at Laura. She could not speak. She wondered if she could summon up the strength to get up and find another compartment — one with other people in it. But even now, even after what had almost happened, *knowing* what Laura had planned, she felt powerless. It was useless struggling now. She felt drugged, poisoned, robbed of all strength to resist.

The train slowed.

They could not sit here silently like this for the rest of the journey. One of them must speak.

A station platform slid gently in beside them. Doors opened and were slammed shut. The corridor door opened, and a middle-aged couple came in. They began to chatter as soon as they were seated, and to the sound of their voices Charlotte dozed off.

10

The telephone tinkled faintly, and then began to ring. It clamoured insistently on both floors, in the consulting-room downstairs and by Doctor Swanton's bedside.

Gil was alone in the house. Doctor Swanton was out visiting a patient, her mother was out shopping, and the other Mrs. Swanton . . . Charlotte . . . well, she was out somewhere too. She had been complaining of not feeling well. Yesterday, Bank Holiday, she had looked pale. Perhaps she had gone out for a walk to make herself feel better. He did not know. He did not let himself want to know.

He went along the landing from his room, and down the stairs. It would not have occurred to him to go to the extension in Doctor Swanton's room.

The rings seemed to get louder and more urgent, and he skidded across the room in order to put an end to the summons.

He said: 'Hello.'

There was a pause, then a doubtful voice said: '*Is* that Doctor Swanton's?'

'Yes, it is.'

'Is the doctor there?'

'No. She's out. She's gone out to see someone.'

'When will she be back?' The voice had become harsh and peremptory.

'I don't know.' Then he remembered the instructions he had been given. He said : 'Can I take a message?'

'I'd sooner . . . ' Again a pause, and a sudden laugh that Gil didn't like. 'Yes, I suppose you could. You can tell her she must come over to Legacy right away. Right away, do you hear?'

'Legacy?' said Gil. 'But I'm sure — I mean, she doesn't have any patients over there. Not that far. Does she?' he added dubiously, not sure whether or not he had overstepped his authority. Laura had told him to choke people off if it were not really urgent, but there were still lots of things she had not made clear to him. 'Is it urgent?' he dutifully remembered.

'Yes. Very urgent. Tell her' — what was

she laughing for, what was the joke? — 'it's . . . Mrs. Swanton. Yes, tell her that. Mrs. Swanton, at the Royal Oak in Legacy.'

'You mean something's happened to her mother — or to . . . ' He faltered for a moment, unable to say 'Charlotte' even to himself, struggling towards 'Mrs. Charlotte Swanton'.

Before he could finish, the hard voice said: 'Not her mother. Just tell her it's Mrs. Swanton, and she'd better hurry. She'd better get here quick.'

There was a click in the receiver, and then the purring sound that marked the end of a conversation. Gil replaced the receiver, and sat down at the desk. He reached for a pencil and put down the message, then studied it. That was the message he had got: he had made no mistake; but what did it all mean?

Something odd had happened a week ago, he knew that. After Mrs. Swanton's absence — the young Mrs. Swanton — there had been something funny in the air. Doctor Swanton had been up to town to fetch her, and everything was queerer than it had been before : there was something awful in the way the two of them walked round one another, treading carefully, not looking at each other and yet being terribly awake.

He did not know what had happened in London. He did not know what had happened now. Charlotte (the name slipped into his consciousness) was up to something. He thought of that man he had seen her with, and tried to push away any idea of what might be going on.

He walked in and out of the different rooms, and stood by the front door for a while, watching for some sign of Doctor Swanton's car returning. She had been gone for ages. There might be something seriously the matter with that Mrs. Swanton. Serve her right if there was — something dreadful, something to do with her being a woman and especially that sort of woman — but she ought not to be kept waiting like this. He wanted to deliver his message and be rid of it.

11

'She said it was about Mrs. Swanton.'

'Mother?' said Laura, one foot out of the car and on the ground.

'No. Just that it was Mrs. Swanton, and she didn't mean your mother. And you'd better get there quick.'

Laura felt a surge of hope that was somehow tinged with frustration. If Charlotte had had an accident, it would remove all risk to herself . . . but she was not sure that the risk mattered so greatly : she *wanted* to be the one who removed Charlotte, wanted to be responsible for her death. A tame, convenient ending now would give her the feeling that she had been cheated.

She said : 'Who made the call?'

'I don't know. She didn't say who she was. She sounded queer.'

Laura rested her weight on the hand that was on the door. She could get out and go indoors and telephone the Royal

Oak. Or she could take in Legacy anyway on the extremity of her own territory: she really owed old Mrs. Neeves on the sluice road a visit, and it would not be too far round.

Gilbert said : 'She sounded as if she was in a hurry. Impatient, like.'

'Oh, all right.'

She drove fast. She visualised Charlotte run over, dying, maimed . . . or ill in some other, more mysterious way.

Or not ill at all. Up to one of her tricks again. Running away, striking out on some fresh stupidity.

But why the summons? Laura could hardly imagine that Charlotte wanted them to have a little heart-to-heart chat before bidding her farewell.

She slewed the car dangerously above Black Waterings, and then picked up speed along the straight stretch below Jury. The town swung slowly to her right, and the hump of Legacy appeared ahead, a hazed silhouette.

Ten minutes more, and Laura was drawing up outside the bulging frontage of the Royal Oak. It was not the best hotel in the town: it sagged over the narrow pavement like a bloated old man on the verge of collapse. The large, low window of the public bar was a hideous frosted green, and the narrow door into the hotel proper no longer fitted its frame.

Just the sort of place Charlotte would choose to meet some man, thought Laura. A place for squalid, furtive pleasure — if pleasure was the word.

She went in. There was a smell of old carpets and upholstery. She crossed the nondescript space that was ncither hall nor lounge, and was going towards the small glass-fronted cubby-hole when a woman came out of the door beside it and intercepted her.

She said : 'So you got here.'

'It was you who sent for me?' said Laura. 'I'm Doctor Swanton.'

'That's right. It was me.'

'Where is Mrs. Swanton?'

She did not know what reply to expect. Perhaps the news that Charlotte was lying dead drunk in one of the bedrooms, or in the bar.

The woman giggled. 'Mrs. Swanton,' she said. 'Yes, I thought that 'ud fetch you.'

Laura stared, dumbfounded.

PART THREE

Then, venom, to thy work.

1

Laura followed the first wardress up the steps, and emerged into the large room with its dark woodwork and bleak, aseptic light. There was a faint rustling and a murmur of voices, stilled at once. She did not look round, but stared impassively at the judge.

The second wardress came up quietly behind her.

The clerk of the court stood below. He spoke to Laura in a solemn voice whose dramatic effect was, for her, ruined by his adenoidal intonation. She listened with professional calm, as though the way he spoke were more important than what he said.

'Laura Felicity Swanton, you are charged on indictment for that you on the 4th day of August in this present year did feloniously, wilfully and of your malice aforethought kill and murder . . . '

It was often like this. There was so

much that she did not need to listen to. And now, although he was addressing her directly and purposefully, she could not take the matter seriously. She was so used to letting people talk without taking too much account of what they actually said.

But now there was a question she must answer. The clerk was challenging her.

She said : 'Not guilty.'

Then she was allowed to sink back into contemplation. She watched the nine men and three women filing into the jury box, and heard them mumbling the oath. ' . . . that I will well and truly try and true deliverance make . . . ' She studied them with dispassionate curiosity. They might have been sitting in her surgery, waiting for her to pass sentence or relieve their fears. That woman on the end there had signs of a thyroid deficiency. The man in the front row, popping a small tablet surreptitiously into his mouth, might be any kind of a hypochondriac. Or perhaps he had a peptic ulcer.

But she was not here to judge them. For once her verdict was not sought. There had been a reversal of the natural order of things, and for once her life was in the hands of others. *They* were the ones who would make the assessment and pronounce the verdict: they were here to judge her.

Not guilty, she had said. And said it firmly, for it was true. She was not guilty. This ritual was a grotesque mockery. How could she, Laura Swanton (Laura *Felicity* Swanton) be declared guilty?

She felt tolerantly sorry for them, wasting their time in this way.

Waste. Of her time and theirs. And of money.

This bewigged creature down there now, for instance. How much money was being wasted by the Crown on the presentation of this case — how much per hour did the services of that portentous man warrant?

'May it please your lordship. Members of the jury, you have heard the charge against the prisoner, and you will be aware that yours is a heavy responsibility — the heaviest that can be laid upon any man or woman. I must lay before you a sequence of facts which will make extremely unpleasant hearing. These facts will, I know, be most carefully considered by all of you, and I am confident that you will in due course agree with the contention of the Crown that the prisoner did commit this appalling murder with which she is charged.

'All murders are appalling. You may feel that one can make no distinction between this murder and any other. Yet I shall unfortunately find it necessary to draw attention to one particularly revolting aspect of this crime which is new in my experience. It will be necessary for you to follow most closely, for on the face of it you may be misled into believing that because the prisoner did not personally administer the poison which resulted in the death . . . '

The sonorous phrases died away into unintelligibility. Laura, seated, slightly in advance of the two wardresses, no longer caught even the vague meaning. Occasionally it seemed that a door opened, and a burst of sound came through; but then it receded again. She tried to concentrate, and could not. She had done nothing but think for the last few weeks, and now somehow, when she sought to be at her most alert, she was incapable of further thought. She was tired.

'It is all the more lamentable' — the counsel for the prosecution had turned away from her, addressing himself earnestly to the jury — 'that this crime should have been carried out by a woman of considerable intelligence and with grave responsibilities towards society. It should hardly be necessary for me to remind you, members of the jury, of the sanctity of the oath which every doctor swears — an oath which the prisoner has seen fit to disregard . . . '

She found herself thinking of Peter. All this was due to Peter. She remembered that day when she had seen him standing in the dock and heard sentence pronounced, and somehow it was far more real than the present scene. What Peter had done was just what she would have expected him to do. And the consequence had been merely a few months in prison. Soon he would be free.

Laura could not let herself think about

the result of this present trial, if the verdict went against her. It was inconceivable.

Peter. He would be free, and of course she, too, would be free — she would be, must be, acquitted — and then somehow they would settle down and everything would be all right.

It had to be, after all that had happened. Events would not have taken this fantastic turn if it had not been for Peter. If he had not been arrested and tried and sentenced, she would not herself be appearing in this court. If there was a logic in that, then continuation of that logic must lead to eventual freedom and happiness for both of them.

'At this point, members of the jury, I feel that I must read to you the prisoner's statement — her signed statement — to the police. It may seem an innocuous document to you. And that is why I must read it. For I propose to call witnesses who will testify that after agreeing to sign this recording of her statement, the prisoner began to cast suspicion on another member of her household. She began, I say, maliciously and cruelly, to imply that this cold-blooded murder was the work of a mere boy. She tried to dissociate herself from all responsibility for providing the poison which caused the death, claiming that the whole situation arose from an error on her part, of which this boy took advantage.

'I fancy that my learned friends for the defence will endeavour to make much of this point. It will be necessary for you to consider every aspect of it most carefully. If you are absolutely convinced that the prisoner's story is true, or — and this is a most important thing, which will be put to you more than once during the course of these proceedings — if you are not absolutely convinced that the prisoner's story is not true, you will of course have no hesitation in acquitting her. It will be my painful duty to endeavour to convince you that the vague implications made against another party are a monstrous fabrication, and that the murder was a calculated deed — a killing evolved by a woman whose profession should have made her, above all things, aware of the sanctity of human life.

'I will now read the first statement which the prisoner made when questioned by the police . . . '

Calculated? thought Laura. The foolish man (what an unfortunate nervous trick he had of plucking at the lank strand of dark brown hair that showed between his wig and his left ear) was making it sound so devilish and methodical. At least, she supposed that was his line of argument. And of course it had been nothing of the sort. She had merely been nudged along by events, and even when the time came to do what she had planned to do, the circumstances had been far from perfect.

Very far from perfect, she thought wryly.

So much fuss over the death of a worthless woman. So much fuss over a . . . well, a mistake. For wasn't that what it was — a mistake?

If they had been trying her for clumsiness, she would have pleaded guilty. She had miscalculated hopelessly. To try her for wanton negligence, for thinking she understood Gil, for acting too quickly and without due consideration for consequences — not working it out like a chess game, and foreseeing where a false move could lead to disaster — yes, it would have been reasonable that they should accuse her of such things.

This other charge was so silly that she could not apply her mind to it.

'And that she, being a qualified medical practitioner' — the voice thundered a sudden denunciation, and an accusing finger pointed at her — 'did have access to such poison . . . '

She wanted to stand up and tell them how silly they were being. It was all a mistake, it had all got twisted. Something different would have happened if only that bottle hadn't been broken. Oh, yes, there would have been a death — certainly, she smiled grimly to herself, there would have been a death — but it would have been in different circumstances. She would not have blundered; she would have acted less impulsively. The bottle had smashed, the beginnings of the idea had stirred, as though the poison itself had begun to burn slowly into activity in her mind, and later she had acted because the opportunity seemed so perfect, so enticing.

If only it were possible to go back and cancel out that false start.

'This boy, Gilbert Drysdale, was on holiday from school during the month of August. He was accustomed to running messages for the prisoner, and delivered medicines to patients or to the office of the local bus company. This is a common arrangement in country practices where a doctor does his or her own dispensing. It was also the practice to leave medicine bottles labelled with patients' names on the ledge in the doctor's waiting-room, to be called for. During this holiday period, Gilbert Drysdale frequently went into the consulting-room to talk to the prisoner. He had been informed by the prisoner, only a few months before, that he was the illegitimate son of her brother, Peter Swanton — who is at present serving a prison sentence — '

'My lord,' protested counsel for the defence, rising, drawing Laura's gaze quizzically towards him, 'I must object to this attempt to blacken the character of the accused by implication — that is, by bringing in irrelevant remarks about her brother.'

The judge leaned forward. 'Has this point which you have seen fit to introduce, Mr. Taplow, a direct bearing on the issue?'

'I can assure your lordship that it has.'

'Very well, Mr. Taplow. Continue. I trust that I shall not be compelled to stop you.'

'I sincerely trust not, my lord. As it happens, the fact of the boy being the illegitimate son of the prisoner's brother, and of that brother being in prison, has an important bearing on subsequent events. We do not know precisely what conversations took place between the boy and the accused, but various witnesses will testify that the accused had proposed certain plans for the boy's future — plans which, as you will realise, might well have been jeopardised if the deceased woman . . .'

If only that bottle hadn't been smashed, thought Laura.

2

Gil propped his bicycle against the wall and went indoors. The back of his shirt clung to him. His face felt suddenly raw now that he was in the house, with its welcome coolness coming to meet him. Wind and sun had scorched his cheeks.

He heard the chinking of bottles in the consulting-room, and then the hiss as the jet from the tall tap struck the sink.

Automatically he pushed his hair back from his damp forehead, and glanced at himself in the mirror above the umbrella stand.

'Is that you, Gilbert?'

'Yes,' he said; and added, with a hesitation that was a fraction less than it had been yesterday and the day before : 'Aunt Laura.'

She did not say anything further as he went in to her.

It was bright in here. The bench and sink gleamed, and the light played across the metallic brilliance of the steriliser.

'Done all the shopping?' said Doctor Swanton . . . Aunt Laura.

'Yes. I'm ready to take the medicines, if there are any.'

'I haven't done them yet. Surgery's only just over. Really, it's as bad as winter, all the petty ailments they've been dreaming up. Bank Holiday hangovers, most of them.'

'Winter?' he said. 'It's awfully hot this morning. It's lovely out.'

She did not look hot. Gil felt that she must know lots of things that only doctors knew — something to take that kept you cool when it was hot, and warm when it was cold.

Remembering, he said: 'Oh, I passed Mr. Howick by the sluice. He said I was to ask you — '

'About Mrs. Howick's indigestion mixture. I know, I know. He's a dreadful fidget, that man. He knows perfectly well I promised to call in this evening.' She opened a round tin, peered into it, and then jotted a note down on her pad. 'I might as well get it done now, though.

But first of all' — she reached for a bottle full of cloudy liquid — 'I'd better see to Charlotte's gripe water.'

Gil said nothing. He looked out of the window at the tamarisks, their pink spikes twitching in the warm breeze.

'She's still lying down upstairs,' said Aunt Laura.

'What's wrong with her?' asked Gil, because he had to say something.

Not that he cared. Lying up there, doing nothing . . . All washed out, lazy, that's what she was.

Aunt Laura said: 'Nothing much. Nothing that you'd be likely to catch, Gilbert.'

He flushed. It must be something womanish, one of those things you didn't mention.

The doctor — his aunt — was busy at the bench, measuring, filling, corking. She mopped up something she had spilt, and then said :

'I've spoken to Mr. Cartwright. And to Dr. Powell over at the Agricultural College. If you work hard when you get back to school, I'm sure you'll be all right. Mr. Cartwright is very pleased.'

The way she spoke, you wouldn't have thought she wanted you to thank her. She had told him already what she was planning for him, just as she might have told him that there was some small job she wanted him to do for her. In the face of such matter-of-factness it was hard to feel excited; yet, as she brought up the topic once more, he did feel the tension in the pit of his stomach which meant that something wonderful — and frighteningly unbelievable — was going to happen. He would get to the Agricultural College after all. If he worked hard, he would get there. And he intended to work hard.

If only she didn't turn away, keeping him at a distance. He wanted to show her how much it meant to him, but he couldn't do it when she was so off-handed.

To go to the College, to learn the things he wanted to learn, to live here in this house with his father and his aunt and . . .

He said: 'But what about . . . what will

she think of it?' He made only the slightest, non-committal movement of his head upwards, but Aunt Laura saw this although she had failed to see the happiness he had tried to communicate to her.

'She won't stop you.'

'No, but . . . well, I mean . . . if my father's here . . . '

Because having his father here had become, obscurely, part of the dream. Aunt Laura herself had made it so. She was the one who had painted it as a wonderful possibility.

If only it had not been for his father's wife. If only she had been . . . well, just *not there.*

Aunt Laura said: 'What do you think about Charlotte? Do you like her?'

He had cooled down since coming into this room, but now he began to feel hot again. Perspiration stood on his skin; his neck became damp.

Aunt Laura was asking too many questions these days. She was talking about personal things, getting close to him. It was like having someone crowding up on you in a bus. She was there, standing over him. First there had been the cool announcement that she intended to keep him on at the school and then send him on to Agricultural College, which gave her a sort of hold on him that he couldn't very well break; then it was 'Aunt Laura' instead of 'Doctor Swanton' or 'miss'; and now she was asking him in that flat voice what he thought about Mrs. Swanton. Several times just lately she had brought Mrs. Swanton into the conversation — Mrs. Swanton, the young one, the one he would no longer name, the one who was idling upstairs. Especially she talked about her when she was telling him of plans for the future. Only a few words each time, but those words were more important than anything else. Gil, she might say, would be going to the College, coming home at week-ends often to see his father . . . and then she would be saying something about his father perhaps not being here, because Mrs. Swanton would have different ideas. After all, she was his wife, and he would have to put her first.

He said unhappily : 'Well . . . '

'Mustn't forget Mrs. Howick, must I?' It was as though he had answered her. She sounded satisfied, and suddenly willing to talk about something else.

She reached for an old-fashioned bottle with a wide, open neck and domed stopper, its label marked in a spidery, faded script. It said: *Tr. Belladonna.* Aunt Laura paused. 'She'll need a fair amount — ten minims to the dose.' She measured out a quantity into the already half-filled medicine bottle on the bench before her, and then held it under the tap until it was full. She pushed the cork in lightly, upended the bottle, and gave it a bang on the bench to drive home the cork.

The dome-shaped stopper of the dispensing bottle quivered, rolled slowly over, and crashed into the sink. It seemed to come apart, not cracking so much as dissolving into fragments.

Gil, glad to be able to do something, came forward to clean up the mess.

'Be careful of the splinters.' Aunt Laura sighed. 'That was the last of my grandfather's bottles. They don't make them like that nowadays.'

He looked at the wide neck. 'We haven't got a cork that'd fit that.'

'No,' she said absently. She, too, was looking at the bottle. Her expression frightened him in some way he could not explain. 'We must decant it into another bottle,' she said, very slowly, as though working something out.

'I'll go and get one of the empties from the store cupboard,' said Gilbert.

'No.' She spoke sharply, but at his stare she recovered herself. 'There's not much left in it. It'll go into a twelve-ounce bottle for now.' She was already transferring the contents of the old bottle while she spoke. 'There. I knew it would just about go in. We must be careful with it, though. It wouldn't do to get it mixed up with another medicine bottle, would it?'

'No,' Gil said.

'I must remember to get some more poison labels.'

He went on looking at the green fluid in the ordinary medicine bottle. 'That's poisonous, is it?'

'Almost everything I've got here is poisonous in large doses. It's all so concentrated. That's why I put such a lot of water in when I'm making up medicines. I've seen the way you've looked at me — don't argue, Gil, you know you have.' She was laughing as she spoke, in a stumbling sort of way. 'As though I was cheating the customer by filling up with water. But if I didn't, there'd be an awful lot of corpses in the Brookchurch area.'

'How — how much of *that* would kill someone?' He nodded slowly at the bottle.

'Hard to say. It's bitter stuff, so I can't imagine anyone would take enough to kill them by accident. I suppose a tablespoon would about do it. It comes' — she seemed to be driven on, wanting to tell him things, to keep talking — 'from Deadly Nightshade, you know.'

'The stuff the kids pick sometimes, and then there's something about them in the papers?'

'We still have our half-dozen deaths a year that way, in this district. The atropine is the poisonous agent. Very hard to detect, too. If someone's poisoned by belladonna, it doesn't show in the way arsenic and that type of metallic poison does. Unless you were looking for it at a post-mortem, you might not find it.'

He could not tell whether she was thinking aloud, telling him something she thought might interest him, or trying to convey something important to him.

'And yet,' he said dully, 'it's a medicine?'

'Most medicines are the same. Take too much, and they can kill you.'

She waved at the array of bottles at one end of the bench, all neatly labelled.

He laughed, although none of it was funny. There was something awfully serious creeping up on him. But he heard himself saying:

'Finishing off a few old enemies, Aunt Laura?'

She nodded approvingly at him. 'Just deliver the knock-out doses to their respective addresses, will you? Never mind Mrs. Howick's — I'll take it in myself this evening.' She glanced at her watch. 'Only half an hour before lunch. There was a big surgery this morning. I can fit one or two of our old chronics in, though.'

The two of them went out companionably into the sunshine. Illness seemed an odd, improbable thing on a day like this. People lying in bed, people suffering, people being a nuisance to themselves and to everyone else . . . It was all wrong. On a day like this you wanted to feel that everything was going to work out wonderfully, and that there would never be anything to spoil it.

'We forgot to do anything about that bottle of belladonna,' said Aunt Laura.

'I'll go back — '

'Don't bother,' she said. It was unlike her to be so slipshod, but somehow he had expected it. 'Remind me this afternoon,' she said, 'to put a proper label on it. We don't want any accidents, do we?'

'No,' said Gil.

3

In this courtroom the past was being gradually reconstructed. The questions, the probing demands and swift challenges, were all meant to evoke the incidents of that past August. Before each witness a picture was summoned up ; some scene was re-created and he was asked to describe the progress of the drama. The whole purpose of a trial was dramatic: it was the equivalent of a play, in which events were presented for the benefit of those twelve solemn-faced creatures in the jurybox.

Presented inaccurately, thought Laura. Distorted, with the wrong emphasis. True and yet not true. True on the face of things but all making the wrong impact.

The court, it had been emphasised in the opening speech for the prosecution, was concerned with matters of fact. And all the facts were there. But they did not add up to what the prosecution claimed they did.

'Call Doctor Francis Whiting.'

Poor Whiting. Laura was amused by the quick apologetic glance he flashed at her. It was hard lines on all of them, having to give evidence against her while she sat and watched. Don't blame me, old Whiting was saying; they're going to ask me what I found, and I shall have to tell them, but there's nothing personal in it. You know me.

She heard him explaining, in his usual hurried, vaguely deprecating way, how he had been called in, why it was he who was called and not the local doctor, and what he found.

The re-creation of the scene — the all-important scene — the dead body in the bedroom . . .

'On the bedside table was a medicine bottle with a label on it, on which the name 'Mrs. Swanton' was written. There was also the printed instruction, 'One tablespoonful four times a day'. The dead woman was lying on the floor. She had been violently sick, and had also suffered from diarrhœa. On examination of the body I found certain symptoms which suggested the possibility of poisoning. The skin was extremely dry, and the pupils were dilated. The police having been sent for, I waited for them to arrive, and reported my opinion that the condition of eyes and skin, together with the vomiting and diarrhœa, were consonant with atropine poisoning.'

Doctor Whiting looked more and more distressed. He answered one or two routine questions, and then stepped down. This sort of thing was not what he was used to. In all his years in the district, nothing like this had ever happened before.

Yet at the same time he was slightly proud as he went away. In spite of the parochial, humdrum nature of his medical practice, he had spotted the symptoms right away. He hadn't thought, as many an old fogey might have done, that the dead woman had just had a stomach upset, or taken some medicine which disagreed with her. He had known at once — he could almost believe he had sensed it in the atmosphere — that there had been foul play. Suicide or murder. He had looked at that body and the mess around it, and had diagnosed atropine poisoning. And he had been right. It was terrible to think of, but at least he had proved what a good doctor he was.

Now there was an expert in the box.

'Am I not right in saying, Sir Everett, that it is harder to detect the presence of belladonna than, say, arsenic, in the human system?'

'Atropine, the active principal of belladonna, is an alkaloid poison. Such poisons do not linger in the body in the same way as the metallic poisons — the minerals — but there are nevertheless quite accurate tests . . . '

The jury listened fascinated to curt technicalities, to stories of drops in cats' eyes. One member of the jury looked as though he, too, might be sick at any moment when the analysis of the dead woman's vomit was described to him.

Really, thought Laura, death is so messy. It was not a new thought to her. She was familiar with the unpleasantness of death's concomitants; but today, unexpectedly, she felt a sympathy for those people who were being forced to consider it for, perhaps, the first time. It was only a momentary flicker; for why should she feel sympathy for those twelve human beings who might prove, in the end, to have no sympathy for her?

'And a fatal dose would consist of . . . ?'

Facts and figures — so compelling, so misleading. Not misleading in the sense that it was not true that the woman was dead. Of course she was dead. Of course she had died of drinking belladonna. One bitter tablespoonful was, as this efficient-sounding man with the Scots burr in his self-satisfied voice was assuring the court, quite sufficient to bring about death. Particularly as the dead woman had been, for one in her condition, undernourished.

The handwriting on the bottle was identified as that of Gilbert Drysdale. The contents were established to be a tincture of belladonna.

Prosecuting counsel was holding forth once more.

'The Crown has called this medical evidence first in order to establish in your minds the assurance that the cause of death was atropine poisoning. It is as well to have this settled at the outset, and it has not been contested by my learned friend for the defence. What we now propose to show you is the means by which this poison was administered. The question of suicide has been raised — it was considered, quite rightly, by the police in the early stages of their investigation. But, as I told you in my opening speech, a letter from Manchester altered their approach.'

Gladys June Bannister was called. She was a small, sharp-featured woman who might have been in her late forties or early fifties. She gabbled the oath with a fierce determination, and glared spitefully at Laura.

'On the 29th of July I got a letter . . . '

The letter was produced for the benefit of the court, and a handwriting expert vouched for its authenticity.

Another scene being conjured up. Another link in the improbable yet terribly convincing story. Laura listened to the hard Northern voice, crackling with a vindictiveness that would have been comic if it had not been so earnest and self-righteous. 'Murderess,' said the voice, grinding out the syllables.

' . . . and then, well, not hearing from her like she said, I got worried, see, and when I saw that bit in the papers I got in touch with the police right away. She ought to have known better. I'd warned her against trying anything like that, and she must have known what a risk she was running, but you couldn't tell her anything . . . '

Laura shook her head, musing. Along with the picture that was being built up for the benefit of the jury, there was another picture in her own mind. She thought, ironically, of Charlotte as she had been up in that bedroom — of the way things had been moving purposefully towards her . . .

4

Charlotte, confined to bed, had been feeling very sorry for herself.

Cystitis, Laura had called it, as though that settled everything. Give the ailment a name, and that was that. 'Quite a common urinary infection,' she had glibly said. That made it no better. It sounded as nasty as it felt. The patient's discomfort and humiliation — for there was something humiliating about it which could not be dismissed by a technical name — meant nothing to the doctor.

Charlotte looked with distaste at the box of pills on her table, and at the medicine bottle. The bottle was almost empty.

She picked up a tattered detective novel which Mrs. Swanton had found somewhere in the house and brought to her. A few pages had been torn out, but this did not seem to make much difference. Charlotte could, in any case, never follow the reasonings of detective inspectors in novels like this — particularly when those inspectors interlarded their deductions with lectures on old lace, the Chinese theatre or the poems of John Donne. It was all too complicated. Every now and then one of the characters would say something which was obviously meant to be terribly significant and which would later prove to be a vital clue; but Charlotte had never been able to retain such items in her mind or fit them into any coherent pattern.

She was instinctively certain that real murders were not like this. Living people were not so ingenious in their methods of taking life. Hitting someone on the head in a rage was an understandable thing: that she could understand, and, indeed, she shivered when she thought how easily she herself might land up in the dock for acting impetuously. There were so many people you felt like hitting on the head. Or shooting someone — that, too, was easily imagined, even though she had never held a gun in her hand. If she ever did get hold of a gun, it would be sure to go off.

But all these red herrings and misunderstandings were silly. She could not be bothered to go on reading. In real life there were surely not these interminable complexities, these innumerable suspects. All the murders you read about in the Sunday papers were brutal and straightforward. There was never any subtlety — only pitifully clumsy attempts to cover the thing up once it was done.

All impetuous and mad . . . like someone pushing someone else out of a railway carriage.

No. She must not think of that. Somehow there had been a mistake. She had been dozing. She could not have seen what she thought she had seen. Laura could not have attempted anything so insane.

She tried to thrust the blurred, nightmarish vision out of her mind. But the printed page before her was no distraction.

She longed for a Sunday paper — for the one Mrs. Swanton got, not Laura's, which was full of articles about solemn books and sour, derogatory reviews of films which Charlotte knew she herself would have enjoyed enormously. It was not as though Laura ever read her paper. It hung about for a couple of days, hardly rumpled, and then was used for lighting the fire.

Today was only Thursday, anyway. Thursday the 4th of August.

It seemed only a short time since those first few days in Brookchurch which she had spent in bed. But then the room had been strange to her, and its strangeness had been a help : she had been saved from despondency by this room and Mrs. Swanton, and by the lazy comfort of those days. She had been wretched at first, but now, when she looked back, they took on an aura of tranquillity. In these new surroundings she had recovered her strength and thought how good and kind people were.

That was before she realised just how much Laura hated her.

Now the room was too familiar. She was trapped. She had got away, but Laura had fetched her back and was imprisoning her. The little room, once so fresh, had become a cell.

That was nonsense. She must not let herself get silly. Below her window she heard Mrs. Swanton's voice, cheerful and inconclusive as ever. Mrs. Swanton would not be a party to keeping her here against her will. If she really thought anything was wrong, she had only to ask Mrs. Swanton to fetch another doctor, to insist on being moved from here — even to get up and walk out, for her illness was not a major one . . . merely depressing, uncomfortable and debilitating.

If only she had something to occupy her mind.

Her eyes strayed to the open page of the detective novel, its spine cracked so that it lay sprawled limply open on the counterpane.

'Detective-Inspector Fennimore raised one patrician eyebrow and said: 'Of course it wasn't a genuine Manet. You spotted that at once, I have no doubt, my good Simpson?''

Oh, *really* . . .

She lay back again, and thought of Peter. Then of Walter. And then, with a vividness that took her breath away, of Peter again.

She wanted Peter. She crossed her hands under the sheet upon her stomach, and felt an awful longing for her husband.

Of course. It was only natural. He was her husband. Nobody else would do.

For one preposterous moment she felt that she was being disloyal to Walter ; and then the absurdity became too much for her, and she laughed out loud. It was a revelation. She was — after all this time it had dawned on her — a faithful wife. Truly faithful. She would not see Walter again.

It was incredible that Walter should so quickly have receded. Only with difficulty could she recall the sound of his voice. Deliberately she tried to evoke the echo of his hoarse, arrogant endearments, and to feel the clutch of his hands. The memory left her unmoved.

Just as the reality had left her unmoved.

Yes, it was true. She had given herself to Walter, driven by her physical need for that ecstasy she had shared with Peter, unable to control herself any longer; and her body had been unawakened. Walter had not assuaged her hunger. There was only one man in the world who could do that now.

She had never expected to turn into a good, faithful wife — it had not been held as an ideal by the circle of people in which she and Peter moved — but now she realised that that was exactly what she was meant to be. It gave her a funny feeling inside. She wanted to tell someone about her discovery because it was so very, very important.

No good telling Walter. Walter would be unlikely to appreciate it.

Poor man, she thought with infinite compassion.

The lovely tranquillity of the revelation was still upon her when footsteps on the landing heralded the arrival of Laura, closely followed by Mrs. Swanton carrying a tray with lunch laid out on it.

Laura looked brisk and determined, her whole bearing announcing that this visit was one of the least of her daily tasks.

'How are we today?' she asked with impersonal cheerfulness, daring Charlotte to say that she did not feel too well.

'Now don't be long,' said Mrs. Swanton, pushing things out of the way so that she could put the tray down. She squinted short-sightedly at the medicine bottle, which she had jarred perilously close to the edge of the table. 'You haven't got much of that left.'

'I've got another bottle made up,' said Laura, bending over Charlotte. 'I meant to bring it when I came up.'

'I'll go and fetch it — '

'No.' Laura straightened up abruptly. 'No, I can send it in later. There's enough for a tablespoonful there.'

Mrs. Swanton began to fuss about the room as though she would gladly stay for some time, putting things straight and then putting them crooked again. As soon as Laura had moved away from the bed, her mother went over to it and tucked Charlotte in, plumping up the pillows and then lifting the tray on to the bed.

'There, now.'

Charlotte warmed to that ready smile and the affection of those fluttering, eager hands.

She said: 'I've been lying here thinking . . .'

'Yes, dear,' said Mrs. Swanton happily. 'It does you good to have a chance of lying back and thinking about things, doesn't it? I wish Laura would put her feet up in the afternoons sometimes.'

'It would probably be a breach of my terms of service with the National Health people,' said Laura, picking up the detective novel and studying the open page with remote contempt.

Charlotte felt that she ought to defend herself by saying that she, too, thought the novel was rubbish. Instead, she said to Mrs. Swanton:

'I do love Peter.'

'Of course you do, dear.'

'I've been thinking about it, and I've just found out how much I love him.'

There were tears in Mrs. Swanton's eyes. 'I'm so glad.' She kissed Charlotte. 'Now get on with your lunch.'

Laura put the book down, She did not appear to have been listening, yet, in her face, there was a disquieting reflection of what Charlotte had seen there once before — in the train, as the door had opened and the wind plucked at her.

But that had been a dream — a dozing, distorted dream.

Downstairs a door slammed.

'Gilbert is back,' said Laura. 'We must go down and have lunch, and leave Charlotte to have hers.'

She nodded, smiling quite affably, as though what she had just heard made everything plain: everything was settled.

At the door she said: 'I'll send you another bottle of medicine up this afternoon.'

'How much more of that horrid stuff do I have to take?'

'Not much more,' said Laura. She held the door open for her mother to go through. 'This should be the last. Perhaps we'll try something a bit different, and see if that will settle it.'

5

He had been asked if he understood the meaning of the oath, and he had said yes. The judge had leaned forward and studied him, asking if he fully appreciated the distinction between right and wrong.

'Read the oath through.'

He had read it through, and it made sense. The judge had asked him one or two more questions, with an expression not unlike that of Mr. Cartwright at his most solemn. But he made you feel steady, in a way Mr. Cartwright never did: he made you sure that he knew what you were doing and what everyone else in this room was doing, and he expected you to play fair.

'Very well. Let the witness be sworn, and we will hear his evidence.'

The oath taken, Gil waited. He was not trembling, but his throat was dry and he hoped he would not sound too funny when he had to answer the next lot of questions. It was as bad as going into class with an excuse for not having done your homework — a good excuse, you thought, but one that old Badger might undermine and work away at until you couldn't remember what story you had started out with.

The tall man in the gown — again like Badger — tugged at a sleeve and smiled up at him.

'Now, Gilbert, you remember what happened in Doctor Swanton's consulting-room on the afternoon of the 4th of August?'

'Yes, sir.'

'Will you tell the court in your own words exactly whar happened?'

Twelve faces stared at him. Gil looked away, but there were other rows of people watching him. He looked at the judge.

'Aunt Laura . . . Doctor Swanton,' he said, 'had broken a bottle in the morning, and the stuff in it — '

'Can you be more specific?' asked counsel. 'Can you say what was in the bottle?'

'Doctor Swanton said — '

'Better if you can tell us without having to quote somebody else,' said counsel, with an encouraging smile. That smile — leading you on, drawing you towards trouble, into saying things that would all add up to what you didn't want to let yourself understand. 'Was there a label on the bottle?'

'Yes,' said Gil. 'It was an old bottle, sort of dark so that you couldn't see into it. And the label said . . . it had a big 'T' and a little 'r', and then 'Belladonna'.'

'Belladonna,' repeated the tall man, with another little flourish of his gown. You expected him to produce a piece of chalk and write the word on a blackboard. 'Belladonna. You are absolutely sure of that?'

'Quite sure,' said Gil.

'All right, then. What did you say happened to this bottle?'

'She knocked the stopper into the sink.'

'Doctor Swanton did?'

'Yes. And it broke.'

'It was an accident?'

'Of course. I mean . . . well, she just banged a small medicine bottle on the bench, and the stopper fell into the sink.'

'Which stopper are you referring to?'

'The stopper of the big bottle — the one with 'Belladonna' written on it.'

'You saw no sign of her *trying* to arrange for the stopper to break? Was it usual for her to place fragile things such as a glass stopper in an unsafe position and then jar the bench so that — '

'My lord, I object.'

Gil, the spell broken, looked from one gowned man to another. He was thankful for a brief rest. Let them argue with one another for a minute. He could not imagine what the trouble was.

'I agree,' the judge was saying. 'You must not lead the witness in that way, Mr. Taplow. Nor must you ask him, even in such a roundabout way, to express an opinion.'

'I am obliged to your lordship.'

The guns were trained on Gil again. *Now! Drysdale! this interesting drama about your French homework being so unhappily mislaid. . . .*

'After the stopper had been broken, what did the accused do?'

Gil looked across at the dock. The accused. The prisoner. It brought the reality sharply home to him. Murder, arrest, prison . . . death. He could not speak. They would be after him if he spoke out the truth, the whole truth, and nothing but the truth. Because it would sound so odd. They would suspect *him*, blame him; and in a way, wouldn't they be right? He had wavered. He had made a muddle of things. It was partly his fault.

Yet Aunt Laura did not look cross. She looked much the same as usual, as though she didn't mind at all, with the usual faintly sarcastic twist to her mouth. She returned his gaze calmly.

'Come, now, will you tell the court what happened when the stopper had been broken?'

There was nothing to do but tell. Gil described the pouring of the belladonna into another bottle that morning; he agreed that it had not been labelled at once, and that instead of being replaced in the poison cupboard it had been left on the bench when the two of them went out.

'That was unusual, was it not?'

'I don't know.'

'In your experience, during the time you had spent with the accused — '

'I don't know,' said Gil wretchedly. 'I was only just beginning to learn where things were kept. I wasn't supposed to touch anything.'

'I see. The medicines were handled entirely by the doctor herself?'

'Yes.'

'At all times?'

'Yes.'

'She never asked you to put any substance in a bottle for her?'

'No.'

'Not even, perhaps, to fill a bottle up with water?'

'No. All she did was give me the bottles when they were ready to go off to the bus or to be delivered to patients.'

'Did you ever write the labels for her?'

Here it came. They were close to it.

'Not often,' he said.

'How often?'

'Only once,' he said.

'When was that?'

Closer to danger he drew. Although he had talked with that solicitor, and he had been told he would be all right if he just said everything straight out, he had not known what it would be like to face this inquisitor. An inquisitor, that's what he was.

It was the afternoon of the 4th of August.

'Aunt Laura — the doctor — was getting some medicines ready for me to deliver. And she . . . '

It was no use trying to put it off. But he wanted to get his breath. He was near the edge: he would have to plunge in, but he must delay it, must have time to summon up the courage to dive down at that cold surface and be engulfed.

'Yes?' said counsel gently.

The water's warm. Come in.

'She got some medicine ready for Mrs. Swanton.'

'Mrs. Swanton? There were two Mrs. Swantons in the house, were there not?'

'Yes.'

'Which one was the medicine for?'

'Well . . . I thought it must be the one upstairs — the one who married . . . my aunt's brother.'

Counsel said: 'Your father, that would be?'

'That's what my aunt told me,' admitted Gil in a low voice.

'There was no other Mrs. Swanton it might have been for?'

'Only the doctor's mother. She was Mrs. Swanton, too.'

'And it couldn't have been for her?'

'She wasn't ill. She hadn't had any medicine before.'

'But the younger Mrs. Swanton *had* been taking medicine before?'

'Medicine and pills,' said Gil. 'She was in bed.'

'Now, when the accused was preparing this medicine — '

'She got it ready in the morning,' said Gil, 'like I told you before.'

'So you did. Thank you. The medicine had been prepared at the same time as the bottle of belladonna was smashed. Or, rather, the stopper was smashed, and the remaining contents of the bottle were poured into a medicine bottle identical with the one in which Mrs. Swanton's medicine had been prepared. Is that right?'

'That's right.'

'Both bottles were still . . . where were the bottles, Gilbert?'

'We'd left both of them on the bench in the morning. When we came in, in the afternoon, after dinner — lunch . . . '

He saw the two bottles. Two ordinary medicine bottles, both filled with a greenish fluid — both looking the same to him, more or less — horrible stuff, so you could easily imagine how bitter it must be.

Aunt Laura was saying: 'We must remember not to mix those up, Gilbert.'

Somehow everything from then on was in slow motion. It took him an age to say:

'Yes, Aunt Laura.'

She took a gummed label out of the wooden compartment in the tray, and uncapped her pen.

'Write it for me, will you? Just put 'Mrs. Swanton' on it.'

'Do you have to write on it even when it's only going upstairs?'

'Professional caution, Gilbert. You must always write on the label.'

He took her pen from her. The printing

at the top of the label said: 'One tablespoonful four times a day.' He put it down on the desk and wrote the two words below it.

'One tablespoon should be enough,' said Aunt Laura abstractedly.

She pushed one of the two bottles towards him.

He licked the label and put it on, smoothing out a wrinkle.

Then she said, still in that measured way: 'Good heavens. That's the wrong one. I'm sure it is.' She uncorked the other bottle, and sniffed it. 'Yes. What a good thing I noticed in time.'

She was gathering up her bag, picking up her appointments book.

He stared at the two bottles on the bench. Poison for Mrs. Swanton. Poison that would remove her — take her right out of the way, so that when his father came home he would come here, because there was no other home. He would come here and not go away again.

That sort of woman . . .

'Don't forget, will you?' Aunt Laura was saying as she went to the door. 'Alter that label over. Write a big label with 'Poison' on it, and stick it on. And then take the proper bottle up to Mrs. Swanton.'

Gil did not move.

'The proper bottle, mind,' said Aunt Laura. 'We don't want any mistakes, do we?'

'No,' said Gil.

She did not even glance at him as she went out.

Everything she had said to him in recent days and weeks came crowding back into his mind. It built up a choking pressure. He knew beyond a doubt that Aunt Laura wouldn't care if he didn't change the labels over. If something went wrong — if *it* happened — it would suit her as well as it would suit him. There would be the two of them and his father, then, just as she had always talked about it. And of course old Mrs. Swanton; but she was all right, she didn't count.

If it happened, Aunt Laura would be the doctor who had to attend the young Mrs. Swanton, wouldn't she? Aunt Laura would do what had to be done — signing certificates, or whatever it was. Somehow she would manage it. She would cover up any mistake made with the bottles.

She had left it all to him. He was alone now.

If it could only happen that he could forget about the bottles. Really forget. Not have to decide anything — just have it wiped from his mind, so that it was all right for him to pick up the bottle of poison and take it upstairs to Mrs. Swanton.

To Charlotte.

He had not let himself think of her by that name for a long time.

It did not conjure up the disturbing picture he had expected. That memory was not as strong and upsetting as it had been.

But it was better, anyway, to think of her as Mrs. Swanton. 'Mr.' or 'Mrs.' anybody . . . that was unreal. They were adults. Give them a name, the name they used among themselves (imagine calling Mr. Cartwright Bertie, which they said was his name) and you brought them down to your own level. You made them real and alive. Charlotte was someone he *knew*.

Someone he had known.

He went towards the bench and looked at his own writing on the label. Mrs. Swanton.

A door opened along the passage, and he heard the other Mrs. Swanton, the old one, singing to herself in a chirping undertone that sometimes rose into a tuneless squeakiness that got nowhere.

He thought that in another minute she would come fussing along the passage, blinking at things, coming in to move a chair an inch one way or the other, making out that she was tidying up after Laura, who never left a thing out of place.

Never. Except those two bottles on the bench.

The footsteps shuffled closer. He reached slowly out towards the bottles.

Mrs. Swanton almost bumped into him as he went towards the foot of the stairs.

'Oh, Gilbert — '

'Won't be a moment,' he said.

He did not look back. A moment later he entered Charlotte's room. He averted his eyes from her, and put the bottle on the table.

And there was a photograph of his father — the sort of photograph he had thought about and wanted to see.

'That's nice of you, Gil, bringing my medicine. Or is it? Horrible stuff.'

He looked at her, and then quickly, again, at his father's photograph. He knew it was his father. He was glad, now, of the decision he had made.

'Isn't it awful,' she said, plucking at his attention. 'Lying here like this — all because of some silly trouble with my waterworks.'

She no longer disturbed him; not as she had once done.

He reached the door.

She said: 'Aren't you staying for just a minute?'

She was wearing a pink nightgown with some frills on the shoulders.

'I've got an awful lot to do,' he said.

'Do sit down. Just for a minute.'

'I think I'd better — '

'I insist.' She reached for the bottle and the spoon. 'We haven't had a chat for ages, have we?'

'No, miss.'

'For heaven's sake, don't be so awkward, Gil. Do sit down.'

He stood where he was, watching as she measured a full spoon of medicine and tipped it reluctantly back. Her mouth opened and she showed her teeth, making one of those exaggerated faces of hers.

'Ugh. It gets worse.'

He turned and went, carrying the picture of her in his head — carrying it clearly into this courtroom where they were asking him questions that seemed to have something to do with her and yet at the same time to be all wrong.

The judge had asked him all that stuff about the difference between right and wrong. Well, he did. He knew. All his doubts had gone, just like that. He had known, suddenly, where he stood.

But the man who had been questioning him didn't want to know about that. The man in the black gown only wanted him to say things about Aunt Laura and things he had seen. What they kept calling facts. Not what anyone said to him, and not what he thought. Those weren't evidence. But without them, the whole truth wasn't the truth at all.

Now there was another man standing up and asking still more questions. This one started out right away as though he didn't believe Gil and wasn't going to believe him.

'You said that you only wrote a label for a medicine bottle once, and that that was on the afternoon of the 4th of August?'

'Yes.' Why go on about it?

'Did you put the label on the bottle yourself?'

'Yes.'

'So that if the two bottles *were* mixed up, it was your fault?'

'Aunt Laura pushed the bottle at me.'

'You did not do it after she had gone?'

'No. She was there. She said — '

'You did not, having discovered that there was a mistake — if, as you say, there *was* a mistake — alter the label over to the right bottle.'

'There wasn't time.'

'How do you mean, there wasn't time? Were you in a hurry to do something else?'

The man kept on about the bottles,

until the place was full of them. Shelves of bottles, cupboards of them. Take one down, put one back. Some of the questions were the same as those the first man had asked, but put in a different way. The first man had seemed to be asking Gil to help him. This one was trying to get him to contradict himself, trying to make out that he was to blame for things. Had he mixed up the bottles by accident, or had he meant to? Had Doctor Swanton really and truly been there at all? Had there been any other witnesses? Was it not true that he, Gilbert Drysdale, had often played in the consulting-room alone, and taken down bottles and looked at them?

'No.' It was not true. He could say so, firmly.

Then there was a question about his father. The first man had been quiet and sympathetic. This one was frowning at him, as though sure there were some dirty secrets to be dug out.

And a question about his mother. One that he could not possibly answer — one that made him shake his head and say

'No, no, I don't know. I *didn't*.'

The prosecuting counsel raised an objection, and the judge began to lecture counsel for the defence. When he had finished, it was like that time when that new maths master got a confidential talk from the headmaster: one of those confidential talks that the whole school knew about. The maths bloke had been subdued after that, but not really much better: he had been more careful, more deadly in a quiet way, more spiteful.

'Is it not true that you had often said to the prisoner that you would like to be in the house just with her and your father?'

'Yes, but — '

'You didn't want anyone else to come along and interfere?'

It was all true, and not true. The right ideas added up to the wrong answers. But he was not allowed to say what was true; and even if he had been able to do so, it could only have made matters worse. That was the awful part of it.

He felt dizzy. He heard the judge saying: 'You need not answer that question if you do not wish.'

He didn't know what he wished. Only to be out of here. He could not be sure which question the judge meant.

Then he was suddenly all right again. The faces came back into focus, and he knew that he must go on — answering carefully, not adding anything, letting them do the work and make a mess of it. If Aunt Laura herself wanted to get up when the time came and tell them what had really happened, that was her business.

Gil looked across at her, half-apologetically, half appealingly.

Aunt Laura was paying no attention to him. She must have lost patience with the long way round they were going. She didn't seem to care what he said. She was not here at all: she was somewhere else, working things out.

6

This was, perhaps, the only scene on which the prosecution's guesses were more or less accurate.

More or less: for no one else had been present, and whatever evidence that interfering woman from Manchester gave, she could still not reproduce the exact conversation that had taken place between Laura and the woman who had summoned her.

Laura half closed her eyes, and was back in the Royal Oak in Legacy. Her attention straying from the steady accumulation of absurd evidence against her, she was back in that drab hall, looking into that woman's face, suddenly remembering.

'Molly,' she wonderingly said.

'Thought the 'Mrs. Swanton' would fetch you. Made you think, didn't it?'

'Actually I thought — '

'Not that I ever really got that far, of

course; but you might say I've got a sort of title to the name. And I thought I'd best not call myself by my own name in case word got round. Wouldn't want to embarrass you.'

Laura had no idea where all this was leading. She was still too surprised to say much or to wonder what all this nonsensical outpouring meant.

'I don't know,' she ventured, 'what your name is now.'

'Same as it always was.'

'Oh. I thought you must have married.'

'Not me. It never did come to that. Not with any of them. Often got a different surname for convenience, but really it's been the same all along. None of 'em lasted long enough for me to get used to 'em.' Her bitterness was half derisive, contemptuous of herself more than of the men. 'Still Molly Drysdale,' she said.

'I see.'

'I thought maybe you'd guess when you got the message. I'm registered here as Mrs. Swanton. It's a common name in these parts — more common than Drysdale. The idea tickled me. But when

I rang up and you didn't answer — some kid was on the phone — '

'Your son,' said Laura.

Molly's face seemed, oddly, to become all at once very round and childish. She gave a nervous little laugh.

'Was it, now?' she said. 'Well. Well, fancy that.' She hesitated, and when she began to speak again she sounded unsure of herself, as though she had forgotten what her motives had been when she telephoned the surgery. 'I thought . . . I'd better ring up. Fetching you over here was best. I didn't fancy coming into Brook-church . . . just in case.'

'In case of what?'

'Just in case. I wanted you to come and see me, and I wondered what you'd make of that. Mrs. Swanton, eh?' Once more the thought seemed to give her childish satisfaction. 'If it wasn't your ma, who else could it be? I thought it'd give you something to think about. I was pretty sure you'd come to check up.'

For a moment Laura did not reply. Evidently Molly was unaware of Charlotte's existence. There was no reason, of course, why she should have known that there really was a Mrs. Peter Swanton now.

Then she said: 'If you really want to talk to me, can't we sit down somewhere? Though I can't imagine — '

'Oh, I've got plenty to talk to you about.'

Now Molly sounded aggressively jubilant, and yet scared. Perhaps no one but Laura would have detected that undercurrent of fear: it was a note she was familiar with, a false harmonic that came into women's voices when they said, 'Well, if you think it's best to let them root about in my inside and see what they can find, I suppose they'd better', or, 'Well, we didn't think of having a baby yet, but we'll manage — just tell me, Doctor . . .'

They went through the door from which Molly had emerged a few minutes before, and entered a small sitting-room with one low window. A door at the other end led into the saloon bar, and beside it was a flight of stairs, open to the room, down which came a persistent draught.

For the first time Laura was able to see Molly clearly.

She felt an immediate glow of satisfaction. Molly had turned out just as she, Laura, had always predicted she would. She looked older than her years, and the slack little mouth had become peevish. Her hair was dyed a rather brassy auburn, though it would have looked quite becoming in its own indeterminate brown shade. Molly was not unlike a faded edition of Charlotte

— the sort of woman, thought Laura, that he had always liked. The soft and pretty, the fluffy and yielding, so soon to become pale and fretful.

Yet as she continued to look at Molly, she saw that this was not altogether true. On that face there were lines and fine fissures cracking faintly under the make-up near her nose; but Molly had not crumpled quite so utterly as Laura had expected. She was still pert and defiant: her voice had its old rasp, her eyes were as arch as ever, and her figure was certainly good.

Laura stared at her appraisingly.

'Well?' said Molly, with a harsh laugh.

'I was just wondering . . . '

'Whether I'm going to have a baby? Well, I am.'

'Splendid.'

It was the nearest Laura ever came to congratulating anyone. 'Splendid' was adequate, so far as she was concerned: she uttered the two syllables with a conventional smile, and that formality was enough.

Although it was not always well received — certain doubts and regrets were often expressed by the glum, expectant mother — the response was rarely in the order of what she now got from Molly.

'Splendid? Not bloody much. What's splendid about it?'

'I was forgetting. You have certain difficulties.'

'That's one way of putting it. I tell you, it's a fine thing, getting caught like this. A fine thing.'

The situation was, in Laura's experience, not an unusual one. It was certainly not the first time Molly herself had been involved.

Laura said: 'I'm sure the father — '

'He's gone,' said Molly. 'Went weeks ago. And I wouldn't want him in on it, anyway; not for the world.'

She obviously enjoyed being melodramatic. It had been not unlike this on that previous occasion, Laura recalled — when it had been a question of Peter's unborn child, the dawning life that was to become Gilbert Drysdale. Then, too, Molly had been exceedingly histrionic. She had run her hand through her hair, wept, and made dramatic gestures — rather repetitious gestures.

It was hard to see why she should have come back to this neighbourhood after so long to repeat the performance.

Laura said: 'I don't see what all this has to do with me.'

'Don't you?'

'I'm afraid not.' She glanced at her watch. 'I'm a long way off my usual round. I really must go.'

'Not yet you don't.'

'I suppose you're after money?'

Molly recognised the sting in the voice, and narrowed her eyes as though to avoid a lash across them.

'I don't want your money,' she flashed out.

There was a footstep behind Laura. She half-turned, and saw a woman standing in the doorway. Her face was familiar — familiar not as that of a patient, but as of someone seen in Jury on market day, or perhaps seen here in Legacy once or twice in five years.

'Oh, sorry,' said the woman, and went out again.

Laura said: 'If you're thinking of coming back to this part of the world . . . ' She had a sudden suspicion that Molly might be wildly dreaming of marrying Peter and settling down here.

'I don't want to stay here, don't you worry,' said Molly. 'Not in this dead and alive hole, thanks. No, I came specially to see you, that's all. To get you to help me.'

'To help you?' She refused to let herself understand.

'You know what I mean.'

This time Laura was on her feet, ready to leave.

'You'd better not walk out now,' said

Molly. 'I'm warning you, you'd better listen.'

Laura stayed, not because of the threat, but because she was so intensely curious to know why Molly thought she had the power to issue threats.

She said: 'Provided you don't make any more suggestions of that sort, which I have no intention of considering — '

'You'd better change your mind about that, Laura. Sit down.'

'I'm perfectly all right where I am, thank you.'

Molly glowered up at her from her chair, and then essayed a conciliatory smile.

'Look, it won't do any good to get mad about it. I'm only asking you reasonably, I don't want to start getting awkward.' She lowered her voice and talked urgently, half appealingly. 'I'm nearly broke. Honest, you've no idea what it's like. I'm not asking you for money . . . though if you want to let me have some afterwards, I won't say no. Never do say no.' The smile flickered hopefully again. 'But I've got to . . . to get rid of this baby. It won't do me any good. And what chance would the kid have? I ask you — what good would it do anyone to have this kid born?'

First Gilbert Drysdale, thought Laura: Gilbert, impinging on her life and on Peter's, Gilbert involved with Charlotte, Gilbert the pointless and unnecessary. And now another human being was forming within this woman.

'I couldn't go to any of those awful old bags in the town,' Molly was saying. 'There was someone in Manchester . . . but the money she was asking, I just couldn't find it, and I wouldn't have gone near her anyway. I used to know someone in London, but she's in jug right now. So then I thought of you.'

'Indeed,' said Laura.

'I thought it'd be just right. There's plenty of people in the district for August week-end — no one'd notice me — and we could get it all fixed up. I can trust you.'

'Not in that way,' said Laura firmly.

'You've got to help me,' said Molly. 'I tell you, Laura, I'm desperate. You can do it all right, and I won't worry you again.

But if you don't . . . '

'Yes?' said Laura. 'If I don't?'

'I'll make a proper scandal. You've kept it dark all these years about me and your precious Peter. First your dad, and then you — you've kept everything nice and sweet and respectable, haven't you? Well, what if I made a fuss now, and let the whole neighbourhood know about it?'

She was almost pushing herself up out of the chair, thrusting herself defiantly at Laura.

Laura said: 'I don't know that it would matter much.'

'Don't try and fool me. I know you lot. Having Peter's name dragged in the mud — and you know what folk round here are. They'd never let you forget it. I tell you, you'll help me or you'll put up with the consequences.'

Laura could not repress a smile. Peter in his northern prison, and this woman talking of dragging his name in the mud!

'You'll be laughing on the other side of your face,' cried Molly furiously.

Laura felt herself withdrawing, back into her own worries. It was useless trying to tell this foolish creature that there were far more important things to worry about than her commonplace misfortunes. Molly constituted no threat whatever. Laura felt, in fact, a twinge of annoyance: she had come here expecting to find Charlotte, expecting to find *something* that would help her to get rid of Charlotte, and all that she had found was this woman and her pitiful blackmail.

She said: 'I'm afraid there's nothing I can do for you, Molly.'

'Oh, isn't there? You can give me something to take. Something to get rid of it.'

Laura shook her head. 'Where did you get the idea that a doctor can 'give you something', as you put it — '

'Don't try that on me. I know you've got plenty of things. And you'd better get busy. I can't hang about here all that long. I'll give you two days at the outside, and if I don't hear from you by then I'll come over to Brookchurch — and let everyone else see me while I'm at it.'

'It won't do you any good,' said Laura indifferently.

'Come off it. You've got to do it for me. And it had better be good. I've left word with a friend of mine in Manchester that if she doesn't hear from me in a week, she's to get in touch with the police.'

'I'm afraid none of this concerns me in the least,' said Laura. She was quite unmoved. This was simply another hysterical patient asking the impossible. She had had so many of them in the past demanding this mythical 'something to take', and would doubtless have many more.

Molly was at a loss. Her face had reddened with anger. She was trying to find something spiteful to say. There must be some way of making this interview run on the lines which she had planned for it.

'It's no good, you know,' she tried wildly. 'You can put on an act now, but you'll climb down soon enough. Because I mean it. You've got to help me.'

'I haven't got to do anything of the sort.'

Laura went to the door. She had had enough of this purposeless conversation.

'When you've thought it over,' said Molly, 'let me know. You can phone me

here. The name is Swanton, remember?'
She laughed harshy. 'Swanton. It ought to
make you think what you owe me — you
and your precious Peter. Better note it
down.'

'I'm hardly likely to need it. Good-bye,
Molly.'

'Once you've thought it over . . . '

Molly's voice, half-threatening and
half-appealing, did not even echo in
Laura's mind. She got back into her car
and turned the ignition key irritably. Time
wasted. Time she could have devoted to
thinking about Charlotte and Gilbert, and
how to get rid of them. Charlotte first.
Charlotte was the important one: Gilbert
was only a pawn, and there must be some
way in which that pawn could be
advantageously moved.

Unfortunately there were other pawns.
There was a move she had not foreseen.

Slowly she drifted back to the present.
The gap was bridged by Gilbert's voice.
She heard him answering a question, and
then she was brought back to awareness
of the court and the ritual that was still
proceeding.

The counsel — prosecutor or defending counsel, she could not for the moment remember which, and was disinclined to make the effort — was asking Gilbert if his Aunt Laura had told him about the existence of his mother. Had she said anything to him about his mother being in Legacy?

'No,' said Gilbert.

'She did not point out to you that your mother might be an obstacle to all the plans that the two of you had recently been making?'

The judge was interrupting. 'What are you trying to prove, Mr. Ferguson?'

'I have been instructed, my lord . . . '

What pathetic delight they derived, thought Laura, from their little exchanges, their tart courtesies.

Why bother; why not finish it all now? She was the one who had instructed the defence to take that line, to implicate Gilbert, because after the first shock of the police inspector's visit and realisation of the net that was closing about her, it had seemed a rather lovely little plan. Her word against Gilbert's: how could she lose? But now she understood, from the very atmosphere of the courtroom, that it stood no chance of success. This long, tortuous argument was a waste of time. It was so terribly obvious that Gilbert was telling the truth. There were other truths he was not telling, but they would be declared irrelevant if he tried to introduce them. Nobody asked him the questions that would open the door to the ironical truth. Nobody asked him whether he considered that Mrs. Charlotte Swanton would impede the fulfilment of his ambitions, of all those things which his Aunt Laura had promised him.

Laura felt as she had felt about Peter when he had stood in the dock. Let them get to the verdict and the sentence; let it be ended. Only in Peter's case there had been no doubt that he had done precisely what he had been charged with doing. In *her* case it was very much otherwise . . .

7

The judge courteously asked the witness if she wished to sit down. She stammered, took off her glasses and wiped them, and then thankfully sat down.

The witness said that she was Isabella Mortlake Swanton and that she was the mother of the accused. On the 4th of August she had gone into the consulting-room at about three o'clock and found two or three medicine bottles on the bench, labelled and with people's names written on them. She had taken these bottles and put them on the shelf in the waiting-room so that they could be collected by the patients for whom they were intended.

Counsel for the defence said: 'Was there anybody else in the consulting-room?'

'No.'

'Was there anybody else in the house?'

'My daughter-in-law was upstairs in

bed, and my grandson' — she said the word defiantly — 'Gilbert had just that minute gone upstairs. I saw him going. He was taking some medicine up to her.'

'You saw him carrying the medicine?'

'I'm pretty sure he had a bottle with him. Anyway, he'd promised that he would.'

'The doctor herself was out?'

'She'd gone out on her rounds.'

'Why did you move the bottles you found: did not the doctor usually do that?'

'Not very often. She was always in such a hurry — in a country place you don't get much chance to potter about the house when folk are sending for you at all hours of the day and night — '

'Quite so. We appreciate that, Mrs. Swanton. So it was usually left to you to put the bottles out on the shelf?'

'Not always me,' said Mrs. Swanton. 'Gil used to do it. But as he was upstairs, and I was tidying the place up anyway, I did it. I used to do it before he came, anyway.'

'You knew the bottles were not

intended for delivery by your grandson on his bicycle?'

'They weren't done up,' said Mrs. Swanton loftily. She cast a glance around the court as though to appeal to everyone to listen to the silly things she was being asked.

'Will you explain that point, please?'

'They weren't done up. I mean, there was a parcel of others in white paper, with a bit of sealing-wax — Laura always did them that way if they were to go by bus or in Gil's saddle-bag.'

'And the bottles you found were not done up in that fashion?'

'I'd have left them, if they had been.'

At this juncture Mrs. Swanton began, for no particular reason, to cry quietly. When she had recovered, angrily jerking her head to make herself stop, counsel went on.

'Now, I want you to cast your mind back, Mrs. Swanton, and think carefully before you answer my next question. Was one of the bottles you picked up standing some distance away from the others?'

Mrs. Swanton took off her glasses and

dabbed at her eyes.

'I think it was,' she said.

'You only think it was: cannot you be sure?'

'Well . . . '

'Please take your time,' said the judge quietly. 'And do not say you are sure merely because you want to finish with the question.'

'I am obliged to your lordship,' said counsel.

There was a long pause.

At last Mrs. Swanton said: 'I think so. But I only think so.'

'I think you will have to leave it at that, Mr. Ferguson,' said the judge.

'I agree, your lordship.' Counsel picked up a scrap of paper, looked at it, and then said: 'Did you read any of the names on the bottles in question?'

'No.'

'Did you ever look at the names on the medicine bottles you handled?'

'Sometimes. When they caught my eye. When it was someone I knew, and I wondered how they were getting on.'

'Your daughter sometimes discussed

patients with you?'

'She was a doctor,' said Mrs. Swanton testily, 'and doctors don't gossip about their patients.'

'Of course not. But if it was a mutual acquaintance, and she was worried about them, did she not occasionally mention the state of their health to you — as a daughter, discussing things with her mother?'

Mrs. Swanton stared. The concept of Laura as a girl seeking advice from her mother, leaning on her judgment, was a new one. She said dubiously:

'Off and on, I suppose. If it was something terribly important.' The idea appealed to her, and she tried to connect it up with some warming incident in her memory. There were so few of them, though. 'If there was anything on her mind,' she valiantly attempted, 'she'd have told me.'

'I'm sure of it. Very natural. Yet although the prosecution claim that she was that day deeply concerned with a threat to the family happiness in the shape of an unexpected intruder, she gave

no sign whatever of any unusual perturbation?'

'None,' said Mrs. Swanton firmly.

'She prepared her medicines in the
usual way, and left the usual bottles on
the bench to be set out for patients to call
for them. Now, Mrs. Swanton: were you
wearing your glasses that day?'

'I don't remember.'

'Is it not true that you are extremely
long-sighted?'

Mrs. Swanton bridled. 'When I was a
girl I had the best eyesight — '

'But today, without your glasses, your
near vision is very poor?'

'Yes.' The admission was grudging.

'If you had been wearing your glasses,
you might have noticed the names on the
labels — you would have recognised
the name of anyone you knew?'

'I suppose I would.'

'If you had seen a label with 'Mrs.
Swanton' written on it you would have
wondered about it, surely?'

'I suppose so.'

'What would have been your idea if you
had seen such a label?'

'I'd have thought it was for Charlotte — my daughter-in-law, who was upstairs.'

'But you had seen your grandson carrying a bottle of medicine upstairs to her.'

'I might have thought he'd taken the wrong bottle. If I'd seen it, I'd have gone up after him.'

'But you didn't see it?'

'No,' said Mrs. Swanton. 'No, that's right. I remember now. I'd left my glasses on the mantelpiece in the kitchen.'

'You are sure of that?'

'Yes.'

Counsel for the prosecution cross-questioned Mrs. Swanton, but in spite of her vagueness and the ease with which she could be thrown into fluttering, confused lamentations, she was positive enough about the essentials. She had not been wearing her glasses — she would swear to that now — she had not seen the names on the labels, she had taken the bottles from the bench and put them on the shelf in the waiting-room . . . and it was all her fault, they had no business to be accusing her daughter of murder when the whole thing was due to her own carelessness.

'If I'd left that lot of bottles, then that awful poison would have still been there when Laura got back, and she'd have labelled it properly . . . it was only because she was rushed off her feet, poor girl . . . '

She was soothed down, and prosecuting counsel asked one or two further questions. Was it not true that Laura was devoted to her brother Peter? Of course it was. They had always been inseparable when they were young. And had she not talked a great deal about the things they would do when he was released from prison? Had she not regularly paid money to Gilbert's grandfather, the late Mr. Drysdale, so that Peter should not be worried?

The question that was not asked was the question that all these others added up to: Was it not true that Laura's devotion bordered on fanaticism, and that she would not stop at murder if she wished to eliminate someone who threatened to interfere in those plans she had

been making for the future? This was not,
could not be, asked directly. But all the
other accumulated questions meant this
and nothing else.

The final witness for the defence was
the accused herself.

8

Examined by Mr. Ferguson, Laura Swanton identified herself and her profession, told the court how many years she had been in practice, and confirmed that her father had been in practice for many years in Brookchurch before her.

'It it a busy practice?'

'Like all country practices, it covers a good deal of ground. I am liable to be called out at any hour of the day or night, and have to travel considerable distances.'

They had rehearsed all this. It was only a matter of remembering her lines, and they seemed so innocuous that this was not difficult.

'You dispense all your own medicines?'

'Most of them. There is no chemist in Brookchurch, and only on special occasions do I send a patient into Jury with a prescription.'

'Have you ever made any serious

mistake in your dispensing through haste or carelessness?'

'Never.'

'Will you tell the court in your own words what happened on the morning of the 4th of August?'

Once again the story, already covered by Gilbert, was told. The breaking of the stopper, the pouring of the belladonna into a twelve-ounce bottle . . .

'And what did you do with the bottle?'

'I put it on the shelf,' said Laura, 'out of harm's way.'

'It has been suggested that you instructed Gilbert Drysdale to write a label bearing the words 'Mrs. Swanton' and that you then confused him so that he stuck the label on the bottle of poison. Is that true?'

'No. It is not true.'

'You are sure you put the bottle on the shelf where it would not be confused with other bottles containing medicine?'

'I am quite sure.'

'Will you explain how the label in the boy's handwriting came to be on the bottle of poison?'

Laura put one hand on the edge of the witness box and held tightly on to it. She took a deep breath.

It was all, really, Gilbert's fault. She ought not to have relied on him. In trying to implicate him, to *let* him be the one who took the poison knowingly up to Charlotte, she had over-estimated her influence on him. It could all have been accomplished so much more smoothly if only events had not conspired to put the provocative idea into her mind. If she had only been content with letting him remain innocent, it could have been done. Or if only he had done what she had expected him to do instead of being a weak, cowardly little fool. If only he had taken that poison up and given it to Charlotte . . .

What then? Laura knew that on that day she had gone out quite sure everything would be all right. It had all seemed neat and foolproof. She would have come back and found the body. She would have cleaned up the mess and called in old Whiting. Tragic. So upsetting, her own sister-in-law.

There would have been few traces of belladonna in the bowel: just enough to justify her admission that she had used a medicine containing belladonna, as was common in cases of gastric trouble. Whiting would not have been suspicious; but even if he had, a postmortem would not have been more than mildly embarrassing. It could all have been glossed over, all plausibly accounted for.

She had been sure of that then, hadn't she?

If only . . .

There were so many regrets. If only she had been able to get some sense out of Gil that afternoon when she had returned and asked where the bottle of poison had gone. It was missing, but he would not tell her what had happened to it. He would hardly speak to her. She should have persisted. But, white-faced, he had said simply, 'I don't know.' There had been loathing in his eyes. He had turned against her; had swung around to fear and hatred of her, renouncing all her plans and all her insinuations, rejecting the insidious idea she had tried to plant in his mind.

'You took Mrs. Swanton's medicine up?' she had calmly asked.

'Yes.'

'And what did you do with the other bottle?'

'Nothing. I never touched it.'

'But it's not here now.'

'Well, I don't know.'

'You must have moved it. Have you broken it?'

'No.'

'Are you hiding it somewhere?' She had infused warmth into her voice, trying to coax out of him some tacit admission that he had not betrayed her but was merely thinking it over, keeping the bottle ready for the time when his courage was ripe.

'No, I'm not. I haven't been in here since you left. I don't . . . don't want . . . '

And then he had run off and left her; and she had been unable to find the bottle.

It had not taken long for its whereabouts to be discovered. The police had not wasted time. First there had been courteous questions, and then the change to stern suspicion. That woman's letter had arrived, and by then it was too late to worry about the things that might have been. She had made a statement, and now the facts must be juggled with so that they would fit in neatly with that statement.

Facts . . . that had led her to this box in a courtroom, with the man who claimed to be defending her blinking owlishly up, waiting for her to reply.

She said: 'The boy was in the consulting-room when I left the house. He could have written out another label and put it on the bottle of belladonna.'

'You mean that he might have done that by mistake?'

'Of course not. He could have done it deliberately, with the intention of giving it to his mother.'

She ignored the gasp that ran round the public benches. She stared straight ahead, her brow furrowed in what might have been taken for austere regret.

'Did he know of the existence of his mother?'

'Yes. I had told him.'

Why should she not say this? It was all

Gilbert's fault. Gilbert had destroyed his own happiness and the happiness of others: why should he not suffer? It was his word against hers.

'Did he know his mother would be visiting the surgery that afternoon?'

Really, for a man who was supposed to be defending her he was being extremely unhelpful. She supposed he would claim that he was trying to elucidate matters.

'I didn't know it myself,' she said, as though she found the question an eminently reasonable one. 'But he may well have decided to take it over on his bicycle and then thought he had had a stroke of luck when she actually appeared.'

The judge leaned forward and made a terse observation about the need for dealing with facts and not with theories.

But she had done what she had to do. Once before she had tried to implicate Gilbert, and he had rejected her. He should not escape so easily this time. She, a doctor of good repute in the district, would surely give more plausible testimony than a boy like Gilbert Drysdale.

She was innocent of this crime. Not,

perhaps, innocent of another, attempted crime; but certainly innocent of this one.

Cross-examination followed the lines she would have expected. Again and again the weapon flashed out, trying to stab her into the admission that she had deliberately prepared poison for Molly Drysdale, that she had told the boy to stick the label on the bottle, that she had, perhaps, told him to take it over to Legacy or else to put it out on the shelf. By whatever means it was meant to reach Molly Drysdale, the intention was certainly — was it not? — that it *should* reach her?

'No.'

She was upright, virtuous, indignant.

Was it not true — here they came again — that she was devoted to her brother Peter? Of course. Would it be true to say that she would have killed anyone who threatened his happiness?

A figure of speech, no more. She was cool — as cool and clear-headed as she had been during the whole course of the trial.

Great play was made in the closing speech for the prosecution of the factor of motive. It was cleverly suggested, though lack of any corroborative evidence made it impossible to say this openly, that Molly Drysdale had probably asked Laura Swanton for money as well as for help in her trouble. And the accused, already saddled with the burden of helping her brother when he came out of prison, and committed to helping young Gilbert Drysdale with his education, had decided to get rid of Molly Drysdale.

Great scorn was heaped on poor, vague Mrs. Swanton, who had, devoted mother that she was, tried to make out that the whole thing was an accident.

The shape of the case, the progression of the arguments . . . these things would be happily assessed by the readers of the evening papers who made a hobby of such things.

The design was worked out. It was interesting to the uninvolved strategist; interesting to make predictions and await their fulfilment.

9

'It is my duty now,' said Mr. Justice Ember, 'to tell you what is the law on the matters which have been put before you, and you must accept my direction without question. The interpretation of the facts and opinions which have been brought forth during this case, and the meaning of the evidence offered, is, however, your responsibility. Having observed the attention which you have all so conscientiously paid throughout this trial, I have no doubt whatsoever that the decision you reach will be a sound one.'

Go on, thought Laura impatiently; go on.

She felt more keyed-up than she had expected. Her fingers twitched, and one side of her face felt strangely frozen, so that she had to keep massaging her cheek with her finger-tips in order to make sure that it was still all right.

She wanted that intolerable man to

hurry on and be done with this pomp and circumstance. How many more times were they going to go over the same ground, prodding at it, turning it over, picking things up and brooding over them?

'If you think,' he was saying, 'that the prisoner intentionally administered belladonna to this woman Molly Drysdale, and that the woman died from the effects of that poison, you must return your verdict accordingly. By 'administered' I do not mean that she did with her own hands give the poison. It is enough that she should have prepared the poison and despatched it to this woman with the intention that the woman should drink it and be thereby killed.

'If you are satisfied that such was not the prisoner's intention, then there is an end to the charge of murder.

'You may wish to accept the suggestion which has been put forward to the effect that the death of Miss Drysdale was due to an extremely careless mistake — or, rather, a sequence of mistakes. It has been suggested that the prisoner, whom various witnesses have declared to be a methodical person by nature — the word 'pernickety' has been used several times — that this normally careful doctor was for some reason negligent on this one occasion, and allowed a bottle of deadly poison to be supplied in place of a bottle of medicine. Should this be your decision, you will realise that criminal negligence on the part of the prisoner is involved, and you may wish — indeed, you are entitled to do so — to return a verdict of manslaughter.

'You have heard it alleged that the prime mover in this case has been not the prisoner but her nephew, Gilbert Drysdale. It has been suggested that this boy took advantage of the prisoner's carelessness on this occasion and deliberately took, or allowed to be sent, poison to his mother in order to prevent her disturbing his present way of life. Quite apart from the vagueness of these suppositions and the likelihood of a boy doing such a thing — and these are matters on which you will certainly make up your own minds — it is my duty to point out to you most emphatically that this court is not putting witnesses on trial. The case is that of the Crown against Laura Felicity Swanton, and you are concerned only with her innocence or guilt. It is not your function to make charges against any other individual or individuals. You are concerned with the prisoner and with nobody else.

'These are matters of law, and it may be necessary for me to give you direction upon them while I am going through the evidence with you. This afternoon we shall go through the evidence together.'

The court adjourned.

After lunch, the jury returned looking as solemn and nobly resolved as they had done on the opening day of the trial. The end was in sight: the symptoms had been explained and argued over, the judge was going to help in indicating the diagnosis, and then they would decide whether the patient was to live or die.

Mr. Justice Ember said:

'It is now my duty to sum up on the evidence. A great deal of the evidence in this case is circumstantial, as the Crown quite rightly pointed out in the opening stages of the trial. Your attention has been directed to a sequence of events prior to the death of Molly Drysdale, and from that sequence you have been asked by the Crown to say that the cumulative effect of these events is so clearly indicative of the guilt of the prisoner as to leave no reasonable doubt in your minds that she was in fact responsible for the administration of poison to Miss Drysdale from which Miss Drysdale died.

'The first question for you is: are you satisfied that there was atropine in the body? By that I do not mean a trace of atropine, but a dangerous quantity. Are you satisfied that the medical evidence offered by the prosecution is accurate and free from prejudice? Doctor Whiting has described the condition in which he found the body when called in by the landlord of the Royal Oak in Legacy, and has told us that at once he suspected, from symptoms which he described, that this woman had died from belladonna poisoning. Two recognised experts, who have no personal interest in the case, have testified that the amount of atropine, the basic poisonous ingredient of belladonna, in the exgurgitated matter was sufficient to form a fatal dose. The defence do not question these findings.

'Now you must ask yourself this very relevant question: are you convinced, beyond the shadow of a doubt, as to who the person was who administered this poison? Perhaps I should put it to you another way. Are you prepared to say with complete certainty that the poison was given to Molly Drysdale by the prisoner?

'The Crown say, and the defence do not deny, that the prisoner had access to such poison. The Crown also make the claim that the prisoner had the opportunity of administering this poison, and had a motive for so doing.

'I must stress here how careful you must be in trying to assess this question of motive. Motive is not intention. Many people in this world have a motive for killing certain of their acquaintances, but this does not mean that they also have the intention of doing so. The fact that there seem to be compelling reasons why one person should kill another gives no legal justification for supposing that such a killing has taken place. You are entitled — indeed, you are morally obliged — when considering the motive for such a crime, to take into account as far as possible the character of the prisoner, as shown either by statements made in this court or on reliable testimony. In this case we have a reputable doctor, well spoken of in the district, known as a conscientious worker, who is declared by the Crown to have had the opportunity, means and motive for administering poison. It is claimed that the prisoner felt an unusually strong attachment to her brother and was looking forward to making a home for himself, his wife and his son when he came out of prison. The arrival of Molly Drysdale may have constituted a threat to all her plans, and she may have been apprehensive of the influence Miss Drysdale would have had on her brother when he was released. There may have been circumstances of which we know nothing: we have only the testimony of one witness in the hotel to the fact that the prisoner and Molly

Drysdale were seen together, and that they appeared to be quarrelling. The prisoner, however, has assured us that she did not take Miss Drysdale seriously — that, in fact, she was so little impressed by Miss Drysdale's threats that she actually forgot all about her for a day or two, and had no intention of assisting her in her scheme for procuring an abortion, and certainly not of murdering her.

'It is claimed by the Crown that the prisoner made up a bottle of supposed medicine with a label bearing the name 'Mrs. Swanton', having arranged for Miss Drysdale to come to the surgery that day to collect it. This apparent medicine was actually belladonna, and the instructions as to the dose were sufficient to ensure that Miss Drysdale would take enough to poison herself. This she would do in the belief that the liquid, whatever it might be and whatever it might taste like, would bring about an abortion. That the unfortunate woman had the intention of attempting this criminal act is borne out by the testimony of her friend, Miss Gladys Bannister, whose communication to the police was a major factor in the instigation of proceedings against the accused. The more worldly among us may feel that no sensible woman would believe that a bottle of medicine would produce the desired effect, but in cross-examination Miss Bannister made it clear that such a delusion is — ah — not uncommon in the circles in which she and the deceased moved. Although the opinions of witnesses must not be taken as evidence, it is not unreasonable to attempt to form a picture of the character of the dead woman from various things that have been said throughout this trial. You are entitled to feel that she was an essentially unpractical, erratic woman — and a gullible one. She believed that medicine would rid her of an unwanted child; and that, of course, means also that she would drink even such an unpleasant-tasting liquid as belladonna without protest, in the belief that its very unpleasantness proved its efficacy.

'It is confirmed by witnesses who have no personal interest in the case that Miss Drysdale left the hotel in Legacy in the late afternoon of the 4th of August, travelled by bus to Brookchurch, and later travelled back to Legacy. Either she took with her the bottle labelled 'Mrs. Swanton', which could have been left on the ledge in the waiting-room, or it was delivered to her later at the hotel.

'It is the contention of the Crown that the prisoner knew of this proposed visit to Brookchurch, and prepared and labelled the poison herself or gave instructions for the bottle to be so labelled. For the defence it is said that the mother admits to having taken several bottles from the consulting-room and placed them on the waiting-room ledge by mistake. It has been established that she is long-sighted, and she has been unable to vouch for the names on any of the bottles concerned that day.

'As to the alternative possibility, that of the bottle of poison being carried by the boy Gilbert Drysdale to the hotel, either knowingly or unknowingly, in the sense that he may or may not have known that it was poison, there is no supporting evidence for this. He declares that he left the poison on the bench and went upstairs with medicine for Mrs. Charlotte Swanton, and that when he came downstairs again he did not go into the consulting-room. His reason for not doing so, although he had been told by the prisoner — or so he said in evidence, and the prisoner has confirmed this — to remove the misleading label from the bottle and substitute one marked 'Poison', was that he felt suddenly frightened of the bottle. You must ask yourselves whether it is reasonable to suppose that a boy of his education should suddenly conceive a superstitious terror of a bottle containing a poison which could not possibly have harmed him unless he deliberately drank it. In doing so, you should bear in mind the irrational fears that do frequently strike children and adolescents. You may feel that the witness was telling the truth. Certainly no one has come forward to say that he was seen cycling into or out of Legacy on that afternoon. His grandmother has testified that she saw him about the house several times and that he would not have had time to get to Legacy and back.

'The boy also insists that he did not

know of the presence in the neighbour-hood of his mother, who had registered herself at the hotel as Mrs. Swanton. When questioned, he has continued to maintain that 'Mrs. Swanton' meant, to him, in connection with the medicine, Mrs. Charlotte Swanton, his father's wife, who was ill upstairs.

'The prisoner, however, says quite plainly that she had told Gilbert about the appearance of his mother. Giving evidence on her own behalf, the prisoner has said that she told the boy . . . '

I wonder why I bothered to do such a silly thing? Laura wondered.

She felt a growing distaste for her own behaviour. Not shame because she had tried to implicate Gilbert, but disgust because she had so signally failed to achieve anything. It had not been worthy of her. To kill for Peter's sake, to alter other people's lives, to scheme and contrive and impose her decisions . . . these things would have been permissible. But to fail, to make such a hopeless mess: that was unforgivable.

'You may think' — the judge's voice

flowed in upon her — 'she is speaking the truth but not the whole truth, and of course it is open to you to think that she is lying. You may find it impossible to believe, for example, that a normally meticulous person such as the prisoner could, on this one important occasion, have been so negligent as to . . . '

She withdrew her attention contemptuously. The result was, to her, no longer in doubt. The lunges forward of the argument, then its qualifying retreats, were turning the minds of the jury in one direction. The judge was expressing himself in his circumlocutory, gently cajoling way — 'direction', they called it! — in favour of a verdict of, at most, manslaughter. And by gently adding the factors of Gilbert's failure to go back into the consulting-room, and Mrs. Swanton's longsightedness, he was suggesting the possibility of a verdict of not guilty on either charge. Not guilty. With, she did not doubt, a very stern reprimand to her for negligence in allowing a deadly poison to be treated so casually. And then, no doubt, trouble with the B.M.A. would follow.

No. She had been wrong. He seemed now to be swinging back in favour of a verdict of manslaughter, without the benefit of the doubt.

'We do not admit the possibility of doubt in decisions made in this court,' he was saying. 'Prisoners are not given the benefit of the doubt. If there is any doubt — any reasonable doubt whatsoever — the prisoner is entitled to an acquittal. You must allow no consideration whatever, no haste or uncertainty or impatience, to influence you into returning a verdict . . . '

She could not any longer bear this inexorable plodding, this ponderous movement towards what must in any case be a wrong decision.

No haste or uncertainty or impatience: she tried to fix on that warning, but it was no use. She gave up. The need to speak came up in her throat like a convulsive cough that could not be denied.

It came home to her with appalling clarity that she had, whatever happened now, lost Peter. She had failed. From lack of planning — even, she wryly thought, from the carelessness of which she had been accused so often during the course of this trial — she had made a gross blunder, and what it all led to was the loss of Peter. If she were to escape scot-free now, he would greet her on his return from prison with a mocking smile. Poor old Laura hauled up before her peers!

Her peers. Those twelve imbeciles who had gaped at her, at counsel, at the judge, and at the ceiling for these interminable days.

They had in some way defiled her. All of them, sitting in judgment on her, had taken liberties which she could never forgive. She fingered her cheek again. Its coldness had become a slimy coldness, as though the contact of so many prying, malicious human beings had left an evil film on her flesh.

Whatever happened, she and Peter could no longer stay in the district. The fabric of her life and her work and her love for Peter was cracking. She could feel the crack running down the centre of her head, widening, every agonising moment. She was in acute pain.

It was as though, she thought, someone

had driven a chisel into her forehead and started prising the two sections apart. Then she laughed to herself. Had not she always refused to take seriously people who found similes for pain? If you had to describe pain, she had pontificated, it was not real.

Then this was not real? No, it was not physical pain: it was impatience, fury, an overwhelming contempt. She was tired of the folly of the world. She hated all the stupid people with whom she had dealt for so long and who now had the impertinence to try and impose their legal rituals upon her. All the imbeciles who would not follow her medical advice, drink the medicines she prescribed, follow the regimen she had laid down for them in order to better and prolong their dismal lives . . . those who did not understand, those who presumed to stand in judgment upon her . . .

Rage welled up within her and drove her up on to her feet.

She did not hear what the judge was saying. She did not want to hear. Instead of talking, he must listen. Incompetence was something she could not tolerate. The thing must be set right. These bewigged actors must learn to play their proper parts, to get the scripts for the right play.

'I won't have it,' she cried out. 'For heaven's sake let's get the charge right. It's not murder of Molly Drysdale, and it's not manslaughter. You've got to start again. The charge is one of attempted murder. The attempted murder of Charlotte Swanton. Swanton, indeed! Too many people calling themselves Swanton who have no business . . .'

The wardresses had seized her arms. She struggled wildly.

The judge was saying: 'I cannot tolerate — '

'Who are you,' she shouted, 'to declare what you won't tolerate? I tell you you're hopelessly wrong. The charge should be one of attempted murder. Let's start again and play fair . . .'

The hands became like vices. She screamed. She could not bear the foul touch of these alien fingers. They left a slime on her that would not come off. For too long she had been handled, prodded, goaded, defiled by these plague-ridden creatures.

In darkness and loathing she went on screaming and struggling, while a great weight seemed to bear down on her and weakness to invade her limbs until at last there was nothing but the darkness.

10

'You mustn't let it upset you,' said Mrs. Swanton. She had been saying it over and over again. 'You're not to let it prey on your mind.'

'Of course not,' said Charlotte flatly.

'You're to forget it. She didn't mean it. You know she . . . she wasn't herself.'

The skies outside were grey, and the wind across the marsh kept striking the house with dogged, insistent blows. Charlotte sat by the window. During the morning she had been seized by intermittent bouts of trembling which she could not control, but now she was beginning to get a grip on herself. The pleading note in Mrs. Swanton's voice ceased to rasp on her nerves. She was able, now, to answer with a reassuring nod.

'She didn't mean all those things she said,' Mrs. Swanton persisted.

Of course Laura had meant them; every word of them. Mad or not, she had meant every word. But one could not say that to her mother: one could only deny it, keeping it at a distance and never mentioning it, hoping that in time the distance would grow greater and greater.

'She only said it,' Mrs. Swanton tried yet another variant of the same appeal, 'because of . . . after she'd . . . broken down.'

'Of course.'

There was a silence during which each of them in her different way gathered strength.

'She would never have said anything like that if she'd been herself.'

Charlotte said: 'It sounds queer, doesn't it — 'During Her Majesty's pleasure'. As though the Queen got some personal enjoyment out of shutting somebody up in . . . in one of those places.'

'It'll all come right in time,' said Mrs. Swanton resolutely. 'We'll have her back when she's better, you'll see. It will all be all right.'

Doubt crept back into her eyes. To have Laura back, at some unspecified time in the future . . . would it in fact be a good thing to have her back?

Charlotte wanted to move across the room and take Mrs. Swanton's hand and kiss her; but that would probably start her off crying again, and Charlotte was not yet ready to cope with that.

'Where's Gil?'

For both of them the thought was a distraction. Charlotte at once got up and went out into the passage. Like Mrs. Swanton, she obscurely felt that Gil ought to be with them.

The consulting-room door was closed. She had a sudden vision of Gil shutting himself in there, taking poison, or blowing the house up. It was a silly, melodramatic idea: but then, there was nothing ordinary in life now; melodrama could lead on to melodrama.

Before she could be snared in yet another agony of doubt and fear, she heard him moving along the landing above.

He came slowly down the stairs.

'Hello, Gil' — her voice seemed to echo, as though the house were quite empty — 'We were wondering where you'd got to.'

'Oh,' he said.

She waited for him to reach her, but although he came down and reached the foot of the stairs he seemed to get no closer to her. His face was set and unyielding. It was not hostile, as it had once been: there was no personal antagonism; but there was something even more alarming in his tenseness than there had been in his adolescent hostility.

'Come on in with us,' said Charlotte.

He followed her, and at once Mrs. Swanton was on her feet, effusive and smothering.

Gil said nothing. He shrugged off the awkward advances of the two women, refusing to be drawn into their company.

'Are you going out for a ride today?' asked Mrs. Swanton at last, helplessly.

'No,' he said. 'No, I don't think so.'

He went out into the garden. He would not go out on his bicycle now, in the public view.

When he had gone, Mrs. Swanton said: 'We can't stay, can we?'

'I haven't thought of it. I don't know.'

'We'll have to move away. Oh, dear . . . I do think it's cruel.'

They could, thought Charlotte, escape. Or she, at any rate, could, in due course. It would not be long now. With remission for good conduct, Peter would soon be free. The two of them could take up where they had left off, as though nothing had happened.

'We must sell the house,' Mrs. Swanton was saying. 'Whoever takes on the practice will need it.'

We . . .

Charlotte felt a need to protest. She did not want to be held responsible for the other Swantons. There were Peter and herself; she did not want to be involved with the problems of anyone else.

But inevitably she tried to imagine what would happen, what it would be like if they all stayed together. To move away altogether, to the city . . . how would that affect Gil? It would deprive him of that deep-rooted connection with the fields and countryside he knew so well, and in which he wanted to work. He would come; he would have to come, and he would find something to do, and he would go on living; but he would not be happy. Yet to stay here was impossible. At the moment they were still recovering from the personal shock of Laura's wild, insane outpourings; but even when the memory of that hideousness was dulled, there would be the eyes and the murmuring voices of the local people to endure — the veiled derision or the intolerable kindness, the awareness of being pointed out and talked about. For Gil, above all, that would be unbearable.

To move, perhaps, to another country town? If too far away, they would be lost: it would take a long time to settle down and be content. But if the town were too near, the murmurs would ripple after them.

Whatever the decision might be, it would involve a great deal of distress and a great deal of organisation and determination.

'Poor Gil,' said Mrs. Swanton, beginning gently to cry.

Poor Gil.

Charlotte was back at the window, staring out into the small garden and watching Gil as he walked stiffly about. He kept his back to the window, which meant that his range was very limited. A few paces one way, then a few back — shuffling rather than walking, looking down into the desolate flowerbeds or up at the fence.

Somehow or other he had to be let out.

She frowned. She wanted impatiently to go right away from this house and leave them to it. It was none of her business. The decision was not up to her. She could not be expected to sort such things out. It was an unfair, unreasonable thing to ask.

'If only Peter were here,' sobbed Mrs. Swanton.

Charlotte knew, and was sure Mrs. Swanton also knew, that Peter would have made no difference. Any decision Peter made would be careless and unhelpful. He would want only to shake off the sense of oppression — to do something, anything, hastily, simply in order to feel that things were moving. 'Let's get things moving,' he would say. And he would give little thought to the direction in which they were moving.

It was no good. Charlotte realised, with a twinge of sheer terror, that it *was* all up to her.

She would have given anything to be able to shake off this growing feeling of responsibility. She had not asked for responsibility, and she had done nothing to deserve it.

But she had married Peter, and was now a Swanton.

If only she had not come here in the first place . . .

But she had come. She had accepted the invitation, and been drawn in. And because of that, a woman had died.

No. She would not accept that. She was the one member of the family free from blame in that terrible affair. She had been ill in bed, she had handled no poison, mixed up no labels, known nothing about Molly Drysdale at all.

But if she had not been here in Brookchurch, if she had never entered this house, then Molly Drysdale would not be dead. Circumstances would have been quite different. Small incidents and hatreds and errors would not have accumulated in the way they had done, things would not have worked out in just the way they had. The woman would still be alive.

And if Molly Drysdale had lived, perhaps there might, in due course, have been other problems.

She must cope with it all. She was the only one who could do so. Mrs. Swanton would be all right: she would talk and weep herself into a recovery, and find a way of going on living without too much pain. But Gil would not find it easy. Gil was blaming himself. Gil would lock up the nightmare inside himself until it grew into something perverted and uncontrollable, unless something were done quickly.

Then there was Peter. She must look after Peter.

The old days were ended. She would never again be able to sit back, waiting for Peter to come home, to give her money and to laugh off everyday troubles, relying on the pleasures and impulses of the moment. She had not just married Peter, as she had thought she was doing: she had married into the Swantons, and they were her concern now. She was the only one capable of making decisions.

It was a task that frightened her, but she must be up to it. She would be.

She half turned towards Mrs. Swanton, as though to begin by putting an end to those convulsive sobs. Then she paused.

Outside was Gil — Gil, with his closed face, Gil with all those things in his mind which must be driven out. She looked at him, standing now quite still with his head down. She saw that this was her major problem. She saw how he would be lost, how he would harden up if she did not soon reach him.

The wind sent a sudden flurry of brittle twigs across the garden, and some of them rapped on the window pane. Gil turned, and looked for a moment at the window.

Charlotte went out of the room and down the passage and out into the garden. He did not move away as she approached; but he did not look up until she spoke. She felt — and prayed that she was right — that his mute stiffness was somehow an invitation, that he was saying to her: Come on. Try. Please try.

She said: 'Gil . . . '

THE END

In the underworld of London, the 'Stranger' controlled the 'Devil's Dozen', a gang noted for the daring and murderous nature of their crimes. However, the Stranger intended to betray his gang members to the police and leave himself with all the proceeds of their crimes. Then one gang member found out the Stranger's plan and his identity — and was quickly silenced. Private investigator Philip Quest was determined to unmask the Stranger. Would he live long enough to do it?

THEY WALK IN DARKNESS

Gerald Verner

Horrifying events in the village of Fendyke St. Mary left lambs with their throats cut. This was followed by the disappearance and murder of six young children — all with their throats cut. Then the bodies of two men and two women were found in Witch's House, a derelict cottage — all poisoned. Yet strangely, the murder had occurred whilst the cottage was surrounded by snow; and after locking the door, the murderer had escaped leaving no tracks . . .